UNDER THE
BRAZILIAN SUN

Roberto de Sousa sat opposite, smouldering in silence again across the table.

'The value is unimportant. The painting is not for resale. My interest is the identity of the artist.' He was silent again, as though turning something over in his mind. 'If you would consent to stay to examine it,' he said at last, 'I would be most grateful—Doctor.'

Her first instinct was a flat refusal. But, conscious that she represented the Massey Gallery, and also deeply curious about the painting and its owner, Katherine changed her mind about a quick getaway. For pride's sake she paused, as though considering her answer, and finally nodded graciously. 'Since you've paid so generously for my time, I have no choice.'

'*Obrigado*, Dr Lister. You shall see the painting in the morning.' He glanced at his watch. 'But now you must be tired after your journey. Please rest before joining me for dinner.'

So she was to have the honour of dining at his table. 'Thank you, Mr de Sousa.'

'*De nada.*'

He escorted her across the hall. '*Ate logo*— until later, Doctor.'

Catherine George was born in Wales, and early on developed a passion for reading which eventually fuelled her compulsion to write. Marriage to an engineer led to nine years in Brazil, but on his later travels the education of her son and daughter kept her in the UK. And, instead of constant reading to pass her lonely evenings, she began to write the first of her romantic novels. When not writing and reading she loves to cook, listen to opera, and browse in antiques shops.

UNDER THE
BRAZILIAN SUN

BY
CATHERINE GEORGE

MILLS & BOON

First published in Great Britain 2011
by Mills & Boon, an imprint of Harlequin (UK) Limited,
Eton House, 18-24 Paradise Road, Richmond, Surrey TW9 1SR

© Catherine George 2011

ISBN: 978 0 263 22062 9

CHAPTER ONE

THE Oporto concourse was crowded, but as Katherine made her way through it with her luggage trolley she finally spotted a man holding up a sign with her name on it.

She smiled politely as she approached him. 'I'm Dr Lister of the Massey Gallery in England.'

The man stared for a moment in blank surprise, then hurriedly took charge of her trolley. *'Bem-vindo, Doutora.* Senhor Sousa sent me to welcome you. My name is Jorge Machado. Please to follow me to the car.'

Katherine was only too pleased to let the man take over. Installed in a sleek limousine she relaxed against the butter-soft leather upholstery as they left the airport to head north into the heart of the Minho, an area of Portugal she'd learned was still deep-rooted in tradition. Once they left the motorway for a slower winding route along the River Lima they passed a cart drawn by plodding oxen oblivious of passing traffic, with two black-clad women pacing alongside, and Katherine smiled in delight. Real Portugal!

Originally, Katherine had intended hiring a car to sandwich in a brief holiday somewhere in the region once her mission was completed, but in the end she had taken her employer's advice and accepted the transport provided. She would simply take a taxi to Viana do Castelo afterwards, and find a hotel for whatever time was left over from her mission. But for now it was good just to sit back and watch this picturesque part of the world go by as she speculated about what waited for her at journey's end.

Some work was necessary, for a start. The unknown Mr de Sousa required an art expert to authenticate a recently acquired painting, and had paid all expenses and fees necessary to fly her boss to Portugal. James Massey was renowned and highly respected in the art world for searching out unrecognised works by major artists, and Katherine considered herself fortunate not only to work at his gallery, but for the benefit of his invaluable experience as he'd taught her how to differentiate between the genuine article and the fake. But James, to his chagrin, had gone down with influenza shortly before he was due to leave for Portugal and had asked Katherine to take his place. Elated that he trusted her to deputise for him, she'd dropped everything to make the flight.

The new man in her life had objected strongly when she put their embryo relationship on hold to take off for Portugal, not least because she turned down his offer to go with her. Katherine had been immovable. A client paying so generously for her services deserved her total concentration. The painting would probably need some cleaning before she could even begin to venture any kind of opinion and, dependent on its age and condition, this might take time. Andrew Hastings had taken the rejection so badly Katherine had been surprised to receive his text at the airport demanding she contact him as soon as she arrived. She shrugged, preferring to think about Mr de Sousa instead. James Massey knew surprisingly little about the client, other than his possession of a painting he believed to be of some importance, and his willingness to pay generously to find out if he was right. She fervently hoped that he *was* right. If the client's find was a dud or, worse, a fake, she didn't fancy breaking the bad news. That was a side of the business normally dealt with by James Massey.

'We have arrived, *Doutora*,' said her chauffeur, and Katherine sat to attention at the sight of high walls with a gated archway surmounted by a stone cross. He aimed a remote control at the wrought iron gates, which swung open to reveal a landscape so beautiful she asked him to drive slowly through acres of rolling verdant gardens ringed with mountain views. When the house itself finally came into view it outdid its surroundings. White-walled and red-roofed, two wings fanned out from a central stone tower wreathed in greenery. Before the car came to a halt in the circular courtyard the massive door in the tower swung open and a plump little woman came hurrying out, her surprise obvious as she set eyes on the visitor.

'Here is Doutora Lister, Lídia,' said Jorge Machado with emphasis on the title as he helped Katherine from the car.

'*Bem-vindo*—welcome to Quinta das Montanhas, *Doutora*,' the woman said, recovering quickly.

Delighted to hear more English, no matter how heavily accented, Katherine smiled warmly. 'How do you do? What a glorious house.'

The woman smiled, pleased. 'Senhor Roberto regret he is not here to greet you but arrives very soon. I take you to your room, *Doutora*.'

Jorge followed behind with the luggage as the friendly, bustling Lidia led Katherine through a vast cool hall with a high vaulted ceiling, and on up a curving stone staircase with a balustrade of wrought iron as delicate as black lace. The smiling woman showed Katherine into a big high-ceilinged room with louvred blinds at tall windows, and an armoire and massive white-covered bed in dark carved wood. And, best sight of all to Katherine at the moment, a tray with an ice bucket and mineral water on a table between the windows.

Jorge followed them to wheel Katherine's luggage to the chest at the foot of the bed, then turned to leave. 'When you are ready, *Doutora*, please to come down to the *varanda*.'

Lidia showed Katherine a door which opened into a bathroom. 'You need, yes?'

'I do indeed. *Obrigada*,' said Katherine in relief, her thanks so fervent the woman smiled in sympathy.

'I bring food now?' she offered, but Katherine shook her head.

'No, thank you; I'm too hot right now. I just need some water.'

Lidia promptly filled a glass for her. 'I come back soon.'

Not sure what "soon" might mean, Katherine downed the water and made do with a wash rather than the shower she would have preferred. She brushed out her hair and pulled it back into a ruthlessly tight twist, and then exchanged her T-shirt and jeans for tailored black linen trousers and plain white shirt. Then with a wry little smile she added the dark-rimmed spectacles she wore for computer work. The efficient look would hopefully impress a man who was bound to be of a certain age if he owned a fabulous house like this *and* had money to spare for valuable paintings. Katherine sent brief texts to James and her friend Rachel, and last, guilty because it was an afterthought, another to Andrew, then began to unpack. Before she'd finished the roar of a car engine shattered the peaceful afternoon and Lidia hurried in, shaking her head in disapproval.

'I do that, *Doutora*. You come now. He is here.'

Katherine followed the woman down the curving staircase and out onto a long veranda with a gleaming floor and carved stone pillars entwined with greenery. A man in A casual linen jacket and jeans leaned against one of them, looking out over the gardens. He was tallish and lean, with a mane of black curling hair and a profile any movie star would have envied. When Lidia spoke he turned quickly, with a smile which died abruptly at the sight of Katherine, his dark eyes narrowed in surprise.

'Doutora Lister,' announced Lidia with a touch of drama and withdrew, leaving total silence behind her.

'*You* are Dr Lister?' the man said at last.

At last, rejoiced her hormones. You've finally found him. 'I'm Katherine Lister, yes,' she said, proud of her composure as she smiled politely.

He sketched a graceful bow. '*Encantado.* Roberto de Sousa. I regret I was not here to welcome you when you arrived.'

'Not at all. Your people made me very welcome.'

The client was a far cry from the elderly businessman Katherine had pictured—at a guess, only a few years older than her own twenty eight. And she could have sworn she'd seen him before somewhere. The overlong hair and dark eyes tilted above knife-edge cheekbones were puzzlingly familiar; unlike the eye-catching scar slashed down one side of his face, which was the once-seen never-forgotten kind. When the silence continued Katherine decided to break it.

'Is there a problem, Mr de Sousa?'

'I was expecting a man,' he said bluntly.

Katherine stiffened. 'I thought Mr Massey explained that he was sending me in his place.'

He nodded coldly. 'He did. But he did not inform me that the expert Dr Lister is a woman.'

'Even so,' said Katherine, every hackle suddenly erect in protest, 'I'm fully qualified to make the inspection you require, Senhor de Sousa. Not with as much experience as Mr Massey, it's true, but with more than enough, I assure you, to give you an informed opinion of your painting.' She waited, but no response was forthcoming. The attraction, it seemed, had not been mutual. 'Of course, if you insist on a male expert I'll leave at once. Though I would be glad of a cup of tea first.'

Roberto de Sousa looked appalled. He clapped his hands, and as if by magic Jorge Machado reappeared, bearing a tray. 'Why has Dr Lister received no refreshment?'

'*Desculpe me, Doutora*,' said the man to Katherine. 'I waited for the *Patrao*.'

'You should have served my guest without waiting for me,' said his employer, frowning. 'Please sit, Dr Lister.'

Jorge filled one of the fragile cups with tea, the other with black coffee, and offered Katherine a platter of cakes she refused with a friendly smile for him as she sat down.

Roberto de Sousa sat opposite, smouldering in silence again across the table. This time, he could just sit there, lip-zipped for ever as far as she was concerned, decided Katherine irritably. Gorgeous he might be, but once she'd drunk the tea she'd ask for transport to Viana do Castelo.

'Please tell me how well you know Mr James Massey,' he said at last.

'All my life,' she said briefly.

'He is a relative?'

'No, just a close friend of my father. How do *you* know him, Mr de Sousa?'

'By reputation and by information I acquired on the Internet. I contacted Mr Massey after my research showed he is the best man to authenticate my painting. I bought it for relatively little—a song, as you say.'

'But you think it's valuable?'

Roberto de Sousa shrugged indifferently. 'The value is unimportant. It is not for resale. My interest is the identity of the artist and, if possible, the subject.' He was silent again, as though turning something over in his mind. 'If you would consent to stay to examine it,' he said at last, 'I would be most grateful...Doctor.'

Her first instinct was a flat refusal. But, conscious that she represented the Massey Gallery, also deeply curious about the painting, Katherine changed her mind about a quick getaway. For pride's sake she paused as though considering her answer, and finally nodded graciously. 'Since you've paid so generously for my time, I have no choice.'

'*Obrigado*, Dr Lister. You shall see the painting in the morning in the full light of day, and tell me your requirements. Mr Massey warned there must be cleaning before any opinion is possible.' He glanced at his watch. 'But now you must be tired after your journey. Please rest before joining me for dinner.'

So she was to have the honour of dining at his table. And the mere mention of dinner reminded her that now her thirst was gone she was hungry. 'Thank you, Mr de Sousa.'

'De nada.' He paused. 'A small thing. If I am addressed correctly it is Mr Sousa.'

'I see. I'll remember that.' She got up.

He escorted her across the hall. *'Ate logo*—until later, Doctor.'

She nodded politely, and mounted the curving stairs with back very erect.

Roberto de Sousa watched her out of sight, then returned, deep in thought, to the veranda. He sat down, absently rubbing the leg which gave him hell if he stood too long. His surprise at finding that Dr Lister was not a man had obviously—and unfortunately—offended his guest. But if she were fully qualified to give an informed opinion on his painting, in theory he had no problem with a female expert. His lips tightened. In practice, however, he deeply resented the need to welcome a woman to his home now he was disfigured; even an efficient intellectual in spectacles like Dr Lister, with her scraped back hair and masculine clothes. At the Quinta the only females in his life were on his staff, whereas at one time he had been surrounded on all sides by beautiful, willing women. His face set in harsh lines as he ran a finger down his scar. All that, and many other things, had changed forever the day his luck had finally run out.

Katherine's equilibrium was in normal working order again by the time she settled down on the bed with a book. Roberto de Sousa's reaction to her had been more of a blow than she cared to admit. Her mane of brown hair and opalescent green eyes were assets which generally did her no harm with the opposite sex. But from the reaction of her client she'd obviously disguised her assets too well in an attempt to minimise the figure which curved a little too much in some places for her own taste, but had never been a drawback where men were concerned. She bit her lip. The client's preference for a male expert was another blow. If she informed Roberto de Sousa that his painting was a fake, or of no intrinsic value, he might refuse to accept her findings. She shrugged. Not the end of the world; she would simply rely on backup from James. Photographs of the painting would be emailed to him for his verdict—and earn her undying gratitude from Judith Massey for keeping her bored, convalescent husband in the loop.

Katherine had wondered beforehand whether she would be invited to join her host's family for the meal, but so far no mention had been made of a wife, or of any other relative. Indeed, James had known so little about the client Katherine had speculated quite a bit about Roberto de Sousa during the flight, but nothing had prepared her for her reaction to him, which was a first in her life when it came to men. She had also been unprepared for his hostility too, which was as surprising as his relative youth and scarred, darkly handsome face. She shrugged. He might have wanted a man to pass judgement on his painting but she would soon show him she was more than equal to the task. Nevertheless, the prospect of dinner was a bit daunting.

Katherine had fully intended wearing a sleeveless leaf-green shift with a clever bit of draping to flatter her curvier bits, but she put it back on its hanger, her eyes glittering coldly as she chose minimising black linen instead. With no jewellery to soften the starkly plain dress and only the merest touch of make-up, tonight she would play the intellectual role to the hilt to dine with a man whose aura of sardonic melancholy was so intriguing—and surprising. She would have expected someone of his age and race to be more outgoing. Perhaps he had been before the scar.

A minute before eight the slightly panting Lidia arrived to announce that Senhor Roberto awaited his guest. Katherine put the glasses on and gave a last look in the mirror to make sure no strand of hair had escaped from its ruthless twist. At last, feeling like Boudicca going into battle, she followed the woman down the curving staircase to the hall, where Jorge was waiting to escort her out on the veranda, which looked even more inviting with soft lights glowing in the greenery wreathing the pillars.

Roberto de Sousa rose slowly from one of the cane chairs and stared at her in total silence, his spirits sinking at the sight of his starkly elegant guest. He recalled himself hurriedly and bade her good evening.

Did he ever say anything without thinking it over first? Katherine wondered.

'Lidia is not pleased because I wished to dine out here,' he said, leading her to a table. 'The *sala de jantar* is big for two people. I thought you would prefer this.' But in truth the preference was his, in the hope that his scar would look less prominent in the soft lighting.

'I do,' she assured him, noting that the table was laid for only two. No wife in evidence then; at least not here.

He pulled out a chair for her. 'What will you drink? Gin and tonic, perhaps?'

Katherine glanced at the frosted bottle sitting in a silver ice bucket. 'May I have a glass of wine?'

'*Pois e.* This is the vinho verde of the Minho.' He removed the cork with a twist of his wrist and filled two glasses. 'I will join you.' He gave her a glass and, reminding himself that she was his guest, touched his own to it. 'What shall we toast?'

'A successful outcome for your painting?'

He nodded. 'To success.'

The cool wine went down like nectar, the perfect accompaniment to the dish of hot appetisers Jorge set in front of Katherine.

'The national dish,' Roberto informed her, '*bolinhas de bacalhau*. You have tasted these before?'

'No, but they smell delicious.' She popped one of the miniature cod balls in her mouth. 'And they taste even better. I'll remember my first food in Portugal with pleasure.'

Roberto sat facing her, his scar stark in his dark face against the white of his shirt, soft lighting or not. 'You have eaten nothing since you arrived?' he said, frowning.

She shook her head. 'Lidia offered, but I was too hot and thirsty.'

'Then you must eat more of these.' He pushed the plate towards her.

'No, thank you,' she said firmly. 'Otherwise I shan't need any dinner.'

'You must eat well, or the chef will take offence.'

The chef! Katherine digested that, along with the *bolinha*, and set out to be a polite dinner guest. 'Have you lived here long, Senhor Sousa?'

'I do not *live* here, Doctor.' He smiled crookedly, the scar much in evidence. 'The Quinta das Montanhas is the retreat I escape to for a holiday alone from time to time.'

Some holiday home! 'This is such a beautiful part of the world,' she remarked, 'but totally unknown territory to me. Unlike the majority of my fellow Brits, I've never been to Portugal before.'

'Then it is most important that you enjoy your first visit.'

Roberto de Sousa, however reluctant, was an attentive host, but Katherine found it hard to relax as they ate crisp grilled chicken fragrant with herbs.

'Is the food to your taste?' said Roberto, refilling her glass.

She nodded politely. 'My compliments to your chef. He's a genius.'

He eyed her in amusement. 'I was joking. Jorge's wife, Lidia, is cook here.'

'Then she's the genius,' said Katherine, and smiled warmly at Jorge as he came to take their plates. 'That was utterly delicious. Please tell your wife.'

He bowed, gratified. '*Obrigado, senhora*. You would like *pudim*?'

Katherine smiled regretfully. 'I can't eat another thing.'

Jorge returned the smile with warmth that won him a wry look from his employer. '*Café, senhora?* Or tea?'

'Not even that, thank you.'

'*I* would like coffee, Jorge, *por favor*,' said his employer sardonically. 'And bring *agua mineral* for the lady.'

'*Agora mesmo, Senhor.*'

Once Jorge was assured later that nothing more was needed, Katherine sat back, gazing out at moonlight which added magic to the scene. 'It's so peaceful here,' she commented. 'I see why you think of it as a haven.'

His eyes shuttered. 'Because I have never stayed here long enough to tire of such peace—until now.' He looked up at her in enquiry. 'I trust that taking Mr Massey's place so suddenly caused no problems for you?'

She shook her head. 'None that I couldn't solve, Mr Sousa.'

'*Muito bem.* I am most interested in your work. What, exactly, do you do at the gallery, Doctor?'

Katherine seized on the subject in relief. 'My job mainly involves searching the Internet for sleepers,' she began, 'the unidentified or wrongly catalogued works that slip through the net unnoticed. It can be very exciting.'

'I hope that my painting is equally so.'

'So do I,' she said with feeling.

'That was a most heartfelt remark!'

She smiled wryly. 'When paintings are brought to us at the gallery, James breaks the bad news when they're copies or fakes.'

He nodded, enlightened. 'And you do not welcome the task of giving me such news.'

'No. I don't.' She looked him in the eye. 'But I will if I have to.'

'Have no fear, Dr Lister. I will not blame you if my painting is a fake. Or doubt your findings,' he added.

'Thank you. I admit that worried me when—' she stopped, flushing.

'When?' he prompted.

'When you were so taken aback because I was a woman.'

'Only because I had been expecting a man,' he said smoothly. 'But if Senhor Massey trusts you to pass judgement on my painting I shall do the same.'

'Thank you!'

'*De nada.* Let me give you more wine.'

'Just water, thank you. I need a clear head for my detective work in the morning.'

His sudden smile altered his face so much it cancelled all impression of familiarity. A smiling Roberto de Sousa was so breathtaking he was definitely like no man Katherine had ever seen before.

'You regard your work as solving a mystery?' he said, intrigued.

'In a way. It's hugely rewarding—and exciting—to reveal the true identity of a lost work of art.'

'Perhaps my painting will be one of these.'

She hoped so. Fervently. 'Do you have any idea who the artist might be?'

'It is more hope than idea. But I shall say nothing until you give me your opinion. Do you rise early?' he added.

'During the working week, yes. I'll start on your painting as early as convenient in the morning.'

Conscious that his initial reception of his guest had been anything but warm, Roberto steeled himself to make amends. 'Before you begin tomorrow, perhaps you would like to explore the gardens—a short walk before your mystery-solving.'

Recognising an olive branch when she saw one, she nodded, smiling. 'I'd like that very much indeed. And now it's time I said goodnight.'

'Your breakfast will be brought to your room. I shall await you here later at nine. Sleep well. *Dorme bem*, as we say in my country.'

She smiled politely. 'My first day in Portugal has been so full I'm sure I will. Now I'm here, I can't imagine why I've never been to your country before.'

'Ah, but Portugal is not *minha terra*, the land of my birth,' he informed her. 'The Quinta das Montanhas is my retreat here in the Minho from time to time, but my family home is in Rio Grande do Sul in the south of Brazil.' He gave her the graceful bow again. 'I am a gaucho.'

She had an instant vision of pampas grasslands and cattle herded by men in flat hats and leather breeches. 'You live on a cattle ranch?' she asked, secretly impressed.

He nodded. 'My father is *patrao*. I rode as soon as I could walk, but long hours in the saddle are not possible for me right now.' His face darkened as he collected a walking stick to cross the hall with her. 'You have noticed I limp?'

'No, I haven't,' said Katherine, surprised, with such obvious truth his face relaxed slightly. 'An accident?'

'A car crash.' He shrugged. 'But, as you see, I survived. *Boa noite*, Doctor.'

It took a long time to fall asleep in the wide bed. Katherine blamed the bright moonlight for keeping her awake, but the real culprit was Roberto de Sousa. She would have been a lot happier about his electrifying effect on her hormones if her impact on him had been anything remotely similar but, mortifyingly, it had not. She felt deeply curious about the accident that had scarred his face and left him with the limp she hadn't noticed until he mentioned it. Other than the scarred, handsome face, her first impression of him had been coordination and grace—plus his obvious displeasure that a mere woman had come to pass judgement on his precious artwork. She sighed, praying that the painting was in reasonable enough condition for any kind of identification, let alone the one he hoped for. In one way she wished James Massey had come here to do it.

But if he had she wouldn't have come here to Quinta das Montanhas and met Roberto de Sousa, the most attractive man she'd ever met in her life, scarred and hostile or not.

She smiled suddenly, imagining the reaction if she described the charismatic client and his glorious house to Andrew Hastings. She'd known Andrew only a short time, but already he was displaying character traits which made it unlikely that their relationship, such as it was, would last much longer. Katherine enjoyed male company, but so far in her life had managed to keep her relationships light and undemanding, firmly second-ary to her work. Orphaned in her teens, she was long accustomed to full autonomy over her life. Loneliness was no problem because she shared the house inherited from her father with two former college friends, both of them male. The three of them lived separate lives on separate floors of her three storey town house, and Hugh and Alastair paid their landlady good money in rent, but Andrew strongly disapproved of the arrangement and had lately begun urging her to share his house instead. Her obdurate refusal was an ongoing bone of conten-tion between them, and her sudden dash to Portugal on the very day that he had tickets for Glyndebourne had been the last straw. But helping James out had been far more important to Katherine than a performance of *The Marriage of Figaro*, gala or not. Besides, she had no intention of moving in with a man whose outlook on life was so different from her own.

In spite of her restless night, Katherine woke early. She had showered and dressed in her usual working uniform of jeans and T-shirt and yanked her hair back in its twist by the time a knock on her door heralded the entry of Lidia with a tray.

'*Bom dia, Doutora*,' Lidia announced, beaming. She put the tray on a small table at the window and drew up a chair.

Katherine returned the smile warmly. 'Good morning, Lidia. *Obrigada.*'

'Is enough breakfast, or you like bacon? Eggs?'

Katherine laughed and assured Lidia that the array of crisp rolls and fruit was more than enough. 'It's perfect. Thank you.'

The woman smiled, pleased. 'Eat well. I come back at nine.'

'Could you ask Jorge to come with you, and take the tripod and work box downstairs?'

'*Pois e.* I tell him.'

With time for the kind of breakfast she never bothered with at home, Katherine sat at the open window to eat at her leisure as she looked out on the acres of beautiful gardens. No matter what happened about the painting, she was glad she'd been given the opportunity to see this heavenly place—and make the acquaintance of Roberto de Sousa. The Gaucho, no less. Very sexy.

The man waiting for her on the veranda later, however, looked weary rather than sexy. The shadowed eyes below the tumble of damp curls conveyed pain to Katherine.

'*Bom dia*,' he said as she joined him. 'You slept well?'

'Very well, thank you.'

Roberto eyed her tripod and work box with interest. 'These are for your work?'

She nodded. 'I take photographs of the painting to record its original condition, and then more shots as I go along. The box contains the various tools and solvents for the preliminary cleaning. This can be a messy process, so I shall need a place to work where I won't spoil anything. And with bright daylight rather than strong sunlight, if possible.'

He nodded. 'I shall arrange it. Do you still wish to walk for a while before you start?'

'Yes, please. I've been gazing out over your gardens while I ate breakfast. I'd love to see more.' And postpone the stress of her first encounter with the painting.

'*Vamos*, then.' He picked up the walking stick leaning against a pillar.

'Are you sure you feel like a walk today?' she asked, and regretted it when his mouth tightened.

'I assure you I can hobble—if that is the word—for a while without falling, Doctor.'

She flushed. 'I'm sorry—'

'No! It is I who am sorry.' He forced a smile. 'Forgive me. I swam too much this morning and now I pay for it. Come. I will show you the pool.'

On the leisurely stroll they encountered two gardeners, elderly men who looked up with smiles as their employer stopped to have a word with them each time.

'They were very pleased to see you,' commented Katherine.

'They have known me all my life,' he informed her. 'Quinta das Montanhas was my mother's childhood home. Now it is mine.'

Katherine was impressed. 'Your mother left it to you?'

'She gave it to me. My mother is still very much alive. But since their marriage, when my father stole her away to live in Rio Grande do Sul, she does not come here often. She dislikes the long flight.'

'I sympathise with her! The flight from the UK to Oporto was more than enough for me. Oh!' she said with sudden pleasure, as they turned down another path. 'A tennis court.'

'You play?'

'Yes, though not very well.'

'Better than I—now,' he said bitterly.

'Forgive the personal question,' she said with caution, 'but can nothing be done for your limp?'

His mouth twisted. '*Deus*, yes! I do the punishing exercises, a physiotherapist tortures me, I swim and walk every day, and every day it is improving. Eventually, I am assured, I shall be normal. Whatever normal may be,' he added savagely. 'To achieve that I shall even endure plastic surgery on my face, so I do not give little children nightmares.'

Mentally kicking herself for bringing the subject up, Katherine was glad to reach the swimming pool, which was big enough to give any man a workout on his daily swim. 'What a wonderful setting, with those trees in the background and the mountains beyond,' she said brightly.

He nodded in brief agreement, but said nothing more until they reached a summerhouse on the way back to the house. 'Before we return, let us inspect the *estufa*. Would this suit for your work? Here you have daylight, no one to disturb you, but you are near the house. Also,' he added, 'it revolves, for you to follow the light.'

Katherine ran up a shallow flight of steps into an octagonal room with a table and wicker chairs, a tiled floor and as much natural light from the windows as she could wish for. She beamed at Roberto. 'This is perfect! All I need now is the painting, plus a large blanket and my equipment and I'll get started.'

'Coffee first,' he said firmly, and waved his stick in the direction of the house. 'We shall drink it on the *varanda*, where the painting awaits.'

It was frustrating for Katherine to keep to Roberto's slow pace. Excitement and apprehension filled her now the moment of truth had finally arrived. Even if the painting was all he believed it to be, she might fail to identify the artist, which would be disaster after insisting that she possessed the necessary expertise. As they mounted the veranda steps the sight of the swathed package on the table accelerated her pulse.

'Shall I unmask him?' asked Roberto.

Katherine nodded, swallowing. 'Yes, please.'

With care, he removed the wrappings from the unframed canvas, then stood back. 'A little dirty, *nao e*?'

'Normal if there's any age to the painting,' she agreed, nerves suddenly gone as she looked down at the canvas, which showed a young dark-haired man in sober eighteenth century clothing. 'Certainly no dandy,' said Katherine slowly, 'though he would look a lot more elegant without the layers of overpaint. The jacket is just a blob and there's too much neck cloth.'

'What does that mean?' demanded Roberto, face tense.

'The overpaint may be hiding a repair in the canvas, or an addition by another artist,' she said absently, her eyes glued to the subject's face, which had suffered less than the body. Itching to get started, she smiled absently at her client. 'If you'll have my gear sent over to the summerhouse—with a thick blanket to lay the painting on, please—I'll get to work straight away.'

'First you must drink coffee,' he insisted as Jorge appeared to place a coffee pot on the waiting tray. Roberto gave him some quick-fire instructions, and the man bore the tripod and work box off to the summerhouse. 'I shall carry the painting there myself when you are ready,' he told Katherine, pulling out a chair for her.

Wishing she could get straight on with the job, she began pouring coffee. 'After I've cleaned the painting with white spirit, I can remove some of the overpaint with solvent, if you wish. By then I might even have some idea about the artist.' She had a pretty wild idea already, but had no intention of dropping names at this stage. Further investigation might prove her horribly wrong, and Roberto de Sousa's faith in her opinion would be gone for good.

He sat down beside her. 'You must not work too long without taking a break. Jorge will fetch you when lunch is ready.'

'I won't be able to face a meal in the middle of the day,' she warned.

'You must eat for energy. A small sandwich, at least,' he said firmly. 'I will join you here at one.' He looked up as Jorge returned. 'All is ready?'

'*Sim, senhor.*'

Katherine found that the summerhouse had already been dusted and swept, and a second table brought in to hold a tray with glasses and bottled water in an ice bucket, also a large metal bell with a wooden handle and a thick brown blanket.

Katherine positioned the blanket where the light was brightest and Roberto laid the painting down on it. He stood back, his eyes on her face as she subjected the painted face to a close scrutiny.

Katherine took her time, her excitement mounting. He looked familiar. Could she possibly be right about the artist?

She turned to smile absently at Roberto. 'Right. I'll make a start now.'

He smiled wryly. 'You wish me to leave you to your detecting, *nao e*?' He touched the bell. 'Ring if you need anything. Jorge will come. I shall see you at lunch.'

Alone with the portrait at last, Katherine took off the spectacles to peer through her magnifying glass. 'Right, young sir. Time for your close up.'

She went over every inch of the painting, then took a photograph to record its original state. Her instinct was screaming at her to start cleaning, but she doggedly kept to her usual routine. Once she'd taken everything she needed from her box, she pulled on a builder's mask and her binocular headband, drew in a deep breath and moistened the first cotton bud with white spirit.

CHAPTER TWO

KATHERINE could have sworn that only minutes had passed when Roberto himself arrived to say lunch awaited her on the veranda, by which time the bin liner at Katherine's feet was piling up with swabs and she was in no mood to break off to eat. But she smiled politely and straightened her back as she exchanged the binocular lenses for her spectacles, aware of his obvious disappointment that she had so little to show for her labours.

'I'm just taking off the dirt. You'll only see a difference when I get to the overpaint.'

'I did not expect him to look worse than before,' he admitted.

'I look worse, too,' she said ruefully as they walked back to the house. 'I need a scrub.'

'I shall wait on the *varanda*,' Roberto said. 'There is no hurry.'

'Yes, there is,' she contradicted. 'I must get back to work.'

His lips twitched. 'You enjoy your detecting so much?'

'I do.' She could have added that in this case it was almost unbearably exciting, but said nothing in case she was wrong.

Over lunch, Roberto told Katherine that he would be out for most of the following day. 'Be sure to stop and rest often. I shall tell Lidia to see to this.'

'Oh, I will,' she assured him.

'Have you any thoughts yet about the hand that painted our young man?' Roberto asked, filling their coffee cups.

'At this stage it's hard to tell. After I've cleaned the canvas I'll remove some of the overpaint to look for signature brush strokes. They function like fingerprints to identify the painter. But I'll only do enough to form an opinion. If the painting is valuable I'll leave the rest to the restorer James uses most, a lady with the necessary experience. Unless there is someone else you have in mind, of course.'

'I have not. It was my intention to leave all in Senhor Massey's hands. But I would trust you to do all, Dr Lister,' he added with formality.

That was a relief! 'It's very kind of you, but I'm an art historian, not a professional restorer. Besides, I can't stay here that long.'

'You are so eager to return to England? You have a lover waiting there for you?' His eyes gleamed as colour rose in her face at the sudden descent into the personal.

'I have a *friend*, yes. But I was referring to my job,' she said frostily.

He raised an eyebrow. 'I am sure Mr Massey would allow you to stay if I asked.'

Katherine finished her coffee and stood up. 'That's up to him.'

'If he agreed, it would cause problems in your private life if you stay here?' Roberto got up more slowly, jaw clenched at the effort.

'None at all.' None that mattered compared to the painting, anyway. She looked at her watch. 'Time I got back to work. I'll just run up to my room for my laptop.'

'I shall see you at dinner. I will not walk with you to the *estufa* because I know well I am too slow for you,' he said sardonically.

Guilty because he was right, Katherine managed a smile. 'I'll look forward to reporting to you at dinner.'

Not as much as I shall, thought Roberto, as he watched her racing up the stairs. His initial hostility towards her was receding rapidly, leaving him with a growing desire to know the efficient Dr Katherine Lister better. The Quinta was a beautiful, peaceful haven, but lonely. He smiled bitterly as he limped back to his rooms. At one time he had longed for privacy and time to himself. His mother had told him many times to be careful what he wished for in case the wish was granted. And, as always, she was right. He would gladly pay James Massey whatever he asked for more of Katherine's time, if only to look forward to conversation with her over dinner. She was a rare type of woman in his experience, expert in the subject which interested him so greatly. And if his scar repelled her she hid it well. He smiled a little. It was unusual to meet a woman who made no effort to use her physical assets to attract him—a novelty compared to the old days. And she had obviously never heard of him, though this was not surprising. His career had been cut short before it reached the heights once hoped for.

Katherine remembered to have a word with Lidia on her way out again, and learned that there was a bathroom on the ground floor for visitors, which would be kept for her sole use during her stay.

'Perfeito!' Katherine said, smiling, having looked the word up in the pocket dictionary acquired for the trip. She settled down to work with new zest now the first stage of cleaning was over.

With a canvas in dirtier condition Katherine would have repeated the cleaning process, but due to the time factor she moved straight on to the next stage. Beginning on a section on the subject's coat, she set down a piece of card with a small window cut in it, then dipped a cotton wool bud in acetone and set to work within the aperture. The effect was electrifying. The overpaint had obviously been applied well within the past fifty years or so because it dissolved like magic within the tiny frame, revealing much lighter pigment underneath. Katherine went on moving the cardboard frame fraction by fraction, applying acetone as she went, and then took a photograph email to James for his verdict, and sat back in one of the chairs for a break.

James rang her almost at once. 'You *are* having an interesting time. That's genuine eighteenth century pigment by the look of it. But ten to one you're going to find damage somewhere. Ask de Sousa whether you should carry on.'

'He's already talking about my staying on here to do that, if you're agreeable.'

'Is he now?' There was a pause. 'As a matter of interest, how old is he, and is there a Senhora de Sousa?'

'He's thirty-something, and if there is a wife she doesn't live here. Bye for now.'

A shadow fell over the steps as she disconnected and Katherine turned, to find Roberto watching her.

'Perdoa-me, it was not my intention to listen, but—'

'You heard what I said.' Her face heated.

He nodded. 'Your lover is jealous that you are living in my house?'

'I was talking to James Massey!'

His face relaxed slightly. 'Your employer was asking about me?'

'Yes. Sorry about that.'

'*Por que?* It is natural he feels responsible for you.' Roberto turned as Jorge arrived with a tray. 'I shall join you here for tea.'

She raised an eyebrow. 'And check on what I've been doing?'

'*Exatamente*,' he agreed.

'It's not a lot. I go very carefully at this stage.'

Roberto leaned to inspect the small area she indicated. 'You photographed only this small section?' he said, astonished, and sat down next to her to look over her shoulder. 'I can see that the paint is lighter there. That is important?'

'Crucial. James agrees that it looks like genuine eighteenth century pigment.' Katherine filled both cups as she began. 'So do you wish to ship the painting to James's restorer right away, or shall I carry on until I have a clearer idea of what's under the overpaint before you send it away for repair?'

'Repair?' he said sharply.

She nodded. 'There may be damage of some kind, rips in the canvas, even holes.'

Roberto blenched. '*Deus!* If so, is repair possible?'

'Oh, yes. The restorer James uses is a miracle worker.'

'But if you remove this overpaint, Katherine, could you then give your opinion on the artist?'

'I could probably do that much, yes. But it would

just be an opinion,' she warned. 'So do you wish me to carry on?'

'Yes. It would please me very much if you continue until our young man is revealed in his true colours. Further decisions can be left until then.' Roberto got up. 'I shall leave you to your detective work.' He turned at the top of the steps. 'When your Mr Massey rings again, tell him the only Senhora de Sousa in my life is my mother. I once had a wife for a short time many years ago it is true, but alas no longer.'

Katherine winced. 'I'm so sorry—'

'No, you mistake me,' he said coolly. 'Mariana is not dead. She divorced me.' His eyes locked on hers. 'Also tell Mr Massey that you are safe here. No harm will come to you in my house.'

Face still hot after he left, she found it hard for a while to resume her usual concentration. Next time James rang she would make sure no one was in earshot. But, to her intense annoyance, it was Andrew who rang a few minutes later.

'Why the hell haven't you called me, Katherine?' he demanded. 'Surely you knew I would be worried?'

'I texted to say I'd arrived—'

'Then obviously forgot all about me!'

'You could have rung me if you were that concerned.'

'It was your place to ring *me*, Katherine, in the circumstances. You took off with barely a word of apology about spoiling the trip to Glyndebourne!'

She gritted her teeth. 'For heaven's sake, Andrew, James was ill and needed me to take his place. It was an emergency! We can go to Glyndebourne any time.'

'I see,' he said stiffly. 'James is obviously far more important to you than I am.'

Enough, thought Katherine. 'I haven't got time for this—'

'No! Please. Don't ring off,' he broke in, his tone suddenly conciliatory. 'I'm sorry, darling—'

'Can't talk any more now; I must get on. Bye.' Before he could interrupt again, she switched off her phone.

Katherine felt so annoyed it took a while to get back into her groove again, but at last she began working at her usual speed, until a combination of fading light and a message from Roberto via Jorge brought her to a halt.

'Senhor Roberto says perhaps finish now, *Doutora*,' said the man tactfully.

Katherine looked at her watch and sat back with a sigh as she removed her goggles and mask. 'I'll just clear up and cover the painting. Can you ask where it should be stored overnight, please?'

'*Sim, senhora*. Then I come back for your equipment.'

'You can leave the work box and tripod here overnight. I'll just take my camera and laptop.' She grimaced as she indicated the overflowing bag of swabs. 'Sorry about the mess.'

He shook his head, smiling. '*Nao importa*.'

Katherine put her solvents and tools back in the box, then put her glasses on and turned back to the painting with mounting optimism. Tomorrow, she promised the young man silently, I'll know for certain who painted you. Maybe—though this is a long shot—I'll even know who you are.

'Dr Lister,' said Roberto, coming up the summerhouse steps, 'you have worked too long—' He stopped dead as he saw the painting.

'Don't worry. I know it looks a mess like that, but by the time I've finished your boy will look a lot better, I promise,' she assured him and began to wrap the canvas very carefully. 'Where will you put him overnight?'

'In the *sala*. Come, I shall show you.' Roberto took the canvas from her so reverently Katherine had to hide a smile.

'When you first saw the painting, what appealed to you about it?' she asked as they crossed the hall. 'It's not everyone's cup of tea.'

'Something about the subject's face called to me very strongly, even through the medium of the Internet. I always visited art galleries whenever I could because painted portraits fascinate me. These days, I visit them through my computer.' He paused before double doors at the end. 'If you will open them, *por favor*, Katherine.'

She went before him into a large, formally furnished drawing room, where the painting to one side of the fireplace caught Katherine's eye. The subject, a young girl in a gauzy white dress, smiled dreamily from the canvas. 'Who is she?'

'I do not know her provenance,' said Roberto with regret. He crossed the room to lay his canvas down on an escritoire. 'The label was "Portrait of a Young Girl", artist unknown, and therefore cost little. She is charming, but to me she looks lonely.'

'So you bought the young man as company for her?'

He nodded. 'He would look good facing her, no?'

'He will do when he's been restored. Have you never researched your pretty lady?'

'No. When I bought her I was *ocupado*—busy—and had no time.'

'Whereas you've gone to great expense as well as time to find out more about your young man!'

Roberto nodded. 'Because I hope I know the artist.'

'Who?' Katherine demanded.

His eyes danced, lighting up his face to an extent which made her blink. 'Ah, no! I await your opinion before I risk mine, *Doutora*.'

'Fair enough—you're paying.'

'Because this is true, I insist you rest before dinner.' He gave her a commanding look. 'Jorge goes with me tomorrow, but I have told Lidia to make sure you do not work too hard while I am gone.'

Had he indeed! 'I get totally absorbed and forget the time,' she admitted. 'But when you see your young man again tomorrow he should look very different. Will you be away all day?'

He shook his head. 'I shall return in time to dine with you.'

'This is a beautiful room,' she remarked as they moved towards the door.

'But formal, no? I prefer my *apartamento* at the back of the house. I can be untidy there without risking Lidia's wrath.'

She laughed. 'That's hard to imagine!'

Roberto nodded in wry agreement. 'I am fortunate such good people care for me.' He paused as he held the door open for her. 'While you are here they will care for you also, and not just because it is my wish. Both Jorge and Lidia think you are a very charming young lady.'

To Katherine's surprise, she felt her face flush. 'How very sweet of them.'

Roberto regarded her with pleasure. '*Que maravilha!* A lady who can blush!'

'Not something I do very often,' she assured him, embarrassed.

'Perhaps it is because you are tired. Rest now. You wish to dine on the *varanda* again?'

'Yes, please.' She walked quickly up the stairs, but this time turned to look down before heading for her room and, to her annoyance, found her face heating again as he gave that graceful bow of his before turning away.

In her room, Katherine stripped off her clothes impatiently. This blushing business had to stop right now. Overpoweringly attractive though her client might be, she was here purely on business. She ran a deep bath instead of a shower and lay back in it, frowning. It was only twenty-four hours since her first encounter with Roberto de Sousa. He had been put out at first because she was a woman, yet now, unless she was mistaken, he was beginning to enjoy her company. Of course that might not be such a big deal from her point of view. Maybe he'd not had much contact with women since his accident, due to the scar he was so bitter about. Yet she was so used to it, already she hardly noticed it. He must have been outrageously handsome without it— probably had to beat women off with a stick. But she was here purely to do a job. And tomorrow, by the time he came home from wherever he was spending the day, she should know whether her instinct was right about the artist. If it was, her job would be done and she could ask for transport to Viana do Castelo as her reward, a prospect which was not nearly as pleasant as it should have been.

A rest on her bed during the day was a novelty to Katherine. A lie in on Sundays was the nearest she ever came to one. But life here at the Quinta das Montanhas was dangerously addictive. It would be all too easy to get into the habit. She wondered if Roberto did the same. He'd mentioned an apartment at the back of the house so perhaps he had a ground floor bedroom—easier for his leg than tackling the beautiful stairs all the time. She was deeply curious to know what had happened, but it was pointless to get too interested in him. Once she'd finished here she would never meet Roberto de Sousa again. Besides, a man who came from a cattle-ranching background in Brazil, with a holiday home like Quinta das Montanhas at his disposal, lived on a different planet from Katherine Lister, art historian and researcher.

This conclusion did not rule out looking a bit more appealing to have dinner with Roberto. Katherine considered the sexy green dress, but in the end went for ivory linen trousers worn with heels and a bronze silk tunic. She let her newly washed hair hang loose to her shoulders, added a touch more make-up than before and, after a moment's hesitation, decided against her glasses. She was ready and waiting when a pretty dark girl knocked on her door.

'Pascoa,' she announced, smiling shyly as she pointed to herself. 'Senhor Roberto waits, *Doutora.*'

'*Obrigada,* Pascoa,' said Katherine, smiling, and followed the girl downstairs to the hall, where Jorge was waiting. 'Good evening,' she greeted him.

'*Boa tarde, Doutora.* Lidia is cooking the *carne de porco,*' he explained as they crossed the hall to the veranda. He opened the doors and ushered her outside. Roberto was leaning in his usual place at a pillar, his eyes on the garden. He turned quickly as she joined him, his eyes wide in involuntary shock which acted like balm on her bruised ego.

'You look…most charming, Doctor,' he said when he'd regained the power of speech. 'It is hard to believe you have been working all day.'

'Not all day. I've been lazing on the bed in the guest

room for the past hour.' She smiled. 'Something I never do at home.'

Roberto pulled out a chair for her and gestured to the wine resting in its silver bucket. 'You would like this again?'

'I would. Thank you.'

'So how do you spend your evenings in England?' he asked as he filled their glasses.

'At home alone, I make supper, do some ironing, watch television or read.' Katherine pulled a face. 'Nothing very exciting.'

'And other times someone takes you out to dinner?' he asked, easing himself down in the chair across the table.

'Yes. Or I go out with friends—female gender,' she added.

'But one of your friends is a man, *nao e*?'

'More than one.' She grinned. 'I share a house with two of them; an arrangement much disapproved of by the man who currently takes me out to dinner.'

Roberto's lips twitched as he offered her morsels of toast spread with paté. 'He is jealous?'

Katherine thought about it. 'Andrew wants me to move into his house instead.'

His eyes gleamed between enviable lashes. 'Do you wish to do that?'

She shook her head. 'Absolutely not. My house really is mine. My father left it to me. And my tenants pay me good rent to share it, and the three of us get together with other friends occasionally for a drink or a meal, which I enjoy very much. Great paté, by the way,' she added.

'*Pate de sardinha*. Lidia made it, so eat more.'

Roberto leaned to top up her glass. 'You say your father left the house to you? He is dead?'

Katherine nodded soberly. 'Yes. My mother died when I was little. Dad brought me up single-handed and did a fantastic job of it.' She cleared her throat. 'Then, just after my eighteenth birthday, he had a major heart attack, which killed him.'

'*Que tragedia*,' he said softly. 'You have other relatives?'

'Dad's younger sister came to live with me at the time, but eventually Charlotte met Sam Napier, the architect she's married to now.' Katherine smiled warmly. 'They wanted me to make my home with them, but though I was deeply grateful to them I preferred to stay on at the house. Two of my fellow students were looking for somewhere to live so, with fantastic help from Sam, modifications were made to create three separate flats. The arrangement works so well Hugh and Alastair are still with me.'

'And you do not wish to leave to join your lover,' he remarked.

'He's just a *friend*,' she said irritably, then caught her lip in her teeth.

Roberto eyed her in wry amusement. 'You do not offend me, Doctor. It is I who do so with my talk of a lover. But that is how this man regards himself, *nao e*?'

'I met him only a short time ago,' she protested.

'It takes only a moment to fall in love!'

She frowned, taken aback by the sudden descent into the personal. 'From impartial observation I've noticed that it takes only a moment to fall back out again, too!'

All talk of love was abandoned as Jorge arrived to

set down a platter of succulent pork slices flanked by an array of vegetables and a side dish of sautéed potato slices.

'This smells heavenly!' Katherine said reverently.

'We shall serve ourselves, Jorge,' said Roberto, and smiled at him. 'Thank Lidia for the *batatinhas*.'

'What are they?' asked Katherine as she helped herself.

'The potatoes.' He smiled. 'They are my weakness prepared this way, but at one time I could not eat as many as I wished.'

'You had to diet?' she said, astonished. 'That's hard to believe.'

'I had to take care with what I ate,' he assured her. 'Now, I do not.'

Katherine longed to know more as she went on with her dinner. 'I always have to watch my weight,' she said sadly.

'*E verdade?*' he said, surprised. 'Why?'

'Otherwise, my clothes don't fit. So, as a basic matter of economy, I try not to eat chocolate, and puddings, and so on.'

Roberto leaned to refill her glass. 'The wine will do no harm, I promise. Not,' he added, 'that I think the *doces* would harm you either, Katherine.' He shot a look at her. 'You allow me use of your name?'

'Of course,' she said quickly, annoyed because she felt flustered. 'I was a bit overweight as a teenager, right up until my father died, when I found that grief was far more effective than any diet.'

His eyes softened. 'You were close to him.'

'Yes. I even followed his career choice. He lectured in art history. He met James Massey when they were at university.'

'And now you work for your father's friend.'

She stiffened. 'Which is absolutely nothing to do with nepotism—'

'I am sure it is not,' Roberto assured her hastily. 'But it would please your father to know that his daughter works in safe keeping with his old friend, I think.'

'True. But I earn my salary, Senhor Sousa.'

He sighed. 'Now I have offended you. *Perdao*! It was not my intention. *Agora*, please eat more or Lidia will also be offended.'

Katherine went on with her meal for a moment or two, then decided to take the plunge. 'May I ask about your accident?'

Roberto tensed as though about to refuse, then shrugged, his eyes bitter. 'I was in a car crash, and fortunate to survive. But for a while it was hard to convince myself of that.'

'Because you were in such pain?'

His smile was sardonic as he refilled their glasses. 'Also because of vanity.'

'*Vanity?*'

Roberto nodded. 'My broken leg was in full length cast, I had bad concussion, black eyes, broken nose and teeth, and half my face held together with stitches. Frankenstein's monster was prettier.'

'Sounds as though you were lucky to be alive,' said Katherine with a shiver. 'Did you have any passengers?'

'*I* was the passenger, Katherine. When the car swerved off the road on a bend the driver leapt clear. The car did not burst into flames as in the movies, *gracas a Deus*, but it suffered much damage as it crashed down a hillside into trees.'

'What happened to the chauffeur?'

His eyes hardened to obsidian. 'The driver was a woman, Katherine. I learned later that she had only a sprained wrist, also *contusoes*—bruises because bushes broke her fall. She ran from the scene in panic. It was left to a passing motorist to ring for help. I knew nothing of this. I woke up in hospital, with my parents by my bed.'

'What a horrible shock for them to see you so badly injured.' Katherine's eyes were warm with sympathy, which hardened to something else entirely at the thought of the woman who'd left Roberto to his fate. 'And the lady driving the car?'

'She rang me eventually at the hospital, begging me to say *I* was driving,' he said without expression. 'But the answer was negative because the police already knew I was not driving. It took much time to free me from the passenger seat of my car.'

'Why would she ask you to do that?'

'We had a disagreement over dinner, and because of it we had taken more wine than was wise, so I insisted on ringing for a taxi. But she was in a great hurry to get away and snatched my keys.' He looked suddenly grim. 'We were still arguing in the car because she would not fasten her seat belt.'

'So she was able to jump clear and leave you to your fate.' Katherine shook her head in disbelief. 'After that, she actually expected you to say you were driving?'

'Yes. But even if I had been fool enough to agree, I could not lie because the police knew the facts, also that Elena had spent the evening with me from the publicity shots taken on our way to dinner. When the truth came out she was fired from a television soap she was appearing in. She had a minor role as an innocent young girl desired by a married man.' He smiled sardonically.

'When it was known that Elena Cabral had not only been drinking but jumped from the car to leave me to my fate, the press crucified her.'

'Where did this happen?'

'Near Porto. There were horrific pictures of me in the press.' His mouth twisted. 'My parents wanted to fly me straight home, but living at the Estancia would have meant much travelling for treatment, so I preferred to remain here to recover in the Minho. My father could stay only a short time with me, but my mother left only recently.' He smiled. 'My parents do not like to be separated for long, so finally I insisted I was well enough for her to leave me.'

Katherine gazed at him in silence. With an Estancia as the family home, the Quinta for holidays, and soap-actress girlfriends in the mix, Roberto de Sousa lived a very different life from hers—or from anyone she knew. 'Thank you for telling me,' she said at last. 'I hope it wasn't painful to talk about it.'

'Not to such a sympathetic listener.' He smiled suddenly, the effect like a light going on in a darkened room. He looked up as Jorge appeared to clear away. 'Tell Lidia the meal was *gostoso*, as usual.'

Katherine nodded in fervent agreement and the man smiled, pleased.

'You would like dessert, *Doutora*?'

'No, thank you,' she said with regret. 'Could I have some tea, please?'

'*Pois e!* I will also bring *café* for the *Patrao*.'

Roberto smiled wryly as the man left. 'I must take the back seat with Jorge now you are here, Katherine.'

She laughed. 'I don't think so. Both Jorge and Lidia obviously think the world of you.'

'My mother told them to take good care of me—and

they do.' He sighed. 'Lidia feeds me well, and Jorge is a slave driver when I exercise, also he will drive me to Viana do Castelo tomorrow for a check-up with a doctor and session with the physio. I prefer to drive myself but for hospital visits Jorge insists he does,' he added loudly as the man came back with a tray.

Jorge smiled. 'Dona Teresa *mandou*,' he said simply.

'He said my mother ordered him to do it, so nothing I say will make any difference,' said Roberto, resigned.

'Thank you.' Katherine smiled warmly at Jorge as he set the tray in front of her.

'De nada, Doutora. Boa noite.'

'So, Katherine,' said Roberto when they were alone, 'will you solve our mystery tomorrow?'

'I certainly hope so, or you'll have spent a lot of money for nothing in getting me here!'

'And will pay more for you to stay longer!' He rolled his eyes. 'That does not sound good, I think. You must make allowances for my English.'

She shook her head. 'You speak it very well. So do Lidia and Jorge to a lesser extent, though with much stronger accents than yours.'

'We sound different because I am Brazilian and I was taught at school. Also I have travelled much. They are Portuguese and have not, but they have learned some basic English to deal with visitors to the Quinta das Montanhas. It is rented out for holidays for part of the year—the reason why I built the pool and the tennis court,' Roberto added.

Katherine stared at him in astonishment. 'You can actually bear to let the general public use your home?'

'When I am not here, yes.' He shrugged. 'I am a practical man, Katherine. People pay very well to stay here, and it provides work for my *empregados* and money for the maintenance of the house. But not so many visitors are booked this season because I stay at the Quinta myself.'

'Does Lidia cook for the guests?'

'I do not allow this. Breakfast only is provided. There are good restaurants in the area.' His jaw clenched. 'For obvious reasons, I do not patronise them.'

'I'm not surprised with someone like Lidia to cook for you!'

He smiled crookedly. 'You do not allow me self-pity.'

'No, indeed,' she said briskly. 'You could so easily have been killed in the accident, yet here you are in this beautiful place, waited on hand and foot.'

'*E verdade*,' he mocked. 'I lack nothing—except company.'

She eyed him warily. 'Surely you could have help with that?'

He shook his head. 'Until now, I felt no lack. I did not realise how lonely I had been until I gained the privilege of *your* company.'

Katherine's eyes narrowed.

'Do not misunderstand,' he said swiftly. 'I am trying to say—very badly—that I would not be human if I did not enjoy the company of a woman who is expert in the subject which interests me most. Who is a most attractive woman,' he added. 'You cannot deny this, Katherine.'

'I'm passable,' she admitted warily.

'But you restrain that beautiful hair and wear severe clothes as disguise.' The dark eyes fastened on hers with intent. 'Have no fear. I expect nothing more than your expertise and your conversation, Katherine.'

'I know that, Senhor Sousa!' she retorted, furious that he imagined she'd thought otherwise.

'Now I have angered you again,' he said, resigned.

Katherine pulled herself together, and returned to safe common ground. 'Reverting to the subject that interests you so much, I find something very familiar about your young gentleman.'

Roberto's eyes lit up. 'You have seen him before?'

'I must have. I certainly know him from somewhere.' She sighed in frustration. 'If James were here he'd probably take one look and instantly tell you the identity of both the subject and the artist, and when and where it was painted.'

He chuckled. 'I am sure Senhor Massey is a most interesting man, but I cannot be sorry that he sent you to me instead, Katherine. Tell me,' he went on, with an abrupt change of subject, 'does this friend of yours ring you every night?'

She blinked. 'No. No, he doesn't. Andrew's not very happy with me right now. I cancelled a night at the opera with him at Glyndebourne so I could help James out by coming here to look at your painting.' Her eyes flashed. 'He feels I let him down.'

Roberto frowned. 'He is a fool, this man.'

'I'm beginning to agree,' she sighed. 'He's charming and good company, but he got hugely stroppy when I insisted that helping James out was far more important than a trip to the opera.'

'Stroppy is angry?'

'Yes, but in a childish way. *Most* unappealing,' she added, eyes kindling.

'So you will not marry him, then.'

'Good heavens, no!' Katherine stared at him, astonished. 'I've never had the least intention of that. Neither has Andrew. My insistence on running my own life would be far too big a problem for him, for a start. And because most men are like him, I don't see marriage in my future at all.'

Roberto nodded morosely. 'Marriage is difficult enough when both partners want the same things. When they do not it is disaster. My wife begged me to give up my way of life for her. When I refused she left me.'

'She didn't like living at your ranch?'

'No.' His eyes shuttered. 'Katherine, will you have a little cognac for a nightcap?'

She shook her head, and refilled her teacup. 'No, thanks. I'll just drink this tea, then I'm off to bed. Shall I give you more coffee, or would it keep you awake?'

'I am not good at sleeping, whether I drink coffee or not.' His mouth turned down. 'And that is fact, not self-pity, Doutora Lister.'

She frowned as she poured. 'Does your leg keep you awake?'

He nodded. 'But it is improving. When I first came here I relied on the *muletas*.' He thought for a moment. 'Supports—crutches, yes? Later, I walked with two sticks, now I need only one. Soon,' he said with confidence, 'I shall walk unaided.'

'Amen to that,' said Katherine gravely, and got up. 'Goodnight, then.'

He rose to his feet with effort he ignored. '*Boa noite*, Katherine. *Dorme bem.*'

CHAPTER THREE

A HARD, exciting day's work, followed by dinner with a host who was no longer so hostile, resulted in such a good night's sleep Katherine woke next morning to find her breakfast had arrived.

Pascoa smiled apologetically as she deposited the tray. '*Bom dia, Senhora*. I wake you?'

'A good thing you did,' Katherine said ruefully, looking at her watch. 'I'm late.'

The girl pulled out a chair. 'Enjoy,' she said shyly.

'I shall. *Obrigada*, Pascoa.'

While Katherine was eating the limousine come into view below her windows and went gliding down the drive. Roberto, it seemed, was already on his way. She felt a pang of sympathy as she pictured the day in front of him. He might not even be up to dining with her tonight, which would be a shame. If her work went really well today, there might not be any other tête-à-tête suppers before she left. Which, for obvious reasons, was probably just as well.

'Senhor Roberto say not work too hard,' said Lidia firmly when she came to collect the tray. She smiled. 'But you will, *nao*?'

'Probably,' admitted Katherine, smiling.

'He left painting on *varanda*.'

'*Obrigada*, Lidia.'

'*De nada.*'

Later, Katherine frowned at the face in the portrait as she laid the painting on the blanket. 'Where *have* I seen you before?' She gathered her tools and settled down to work, her excitement mounting as she gradually revealed folds in the man's coat. She let out a whistle when she removed the overpaint from the cravat and discovered not only a more modest neck cloth, but a series of small rips, roughly sealed with filler. Confident that James' favourite restorer would deal with those, Katherine carried on undeterred, eager to get to the face. Lidia brought her back to earth with a jolt a few minutes later when she arrived with a coffee tray.

'Rest now, *Doutora*,' she said firmly.

Katherine stretched, feeling guilty when she looked at her watch. 'Is that the time already?'

Lidia smiled as she poured coffee. 'You love your work.'

'I do indeed.' She drank gratefully. 'Wonderful. I needed that.'

'Lunch *numa hora*,' said the woman, holding up one finger.

A phone call from Andrew interrupted Katherine soon afterwards.

'Hi,' she said briefly.

'Ah, the elusive Dr Lister herself,' he said with sarcasm. 'You've actually deigned to answer your phone.'

'I had forgotten to turn it on—sorry.'

'So you should be. I was worried, woman!'

Woman? 'Absolutely no need, Andrew. I'm just caught up in the work I'm doing here.'

'Revealing a lost Rembrandt to the world, I suppose!'

Her eyes flashed coldly at the sneer in his voice. 'No. Not a Rembrandt—but something very interesting, just the same, both to me and the client. Look, I'm at a rather tricky stage right now.'

'Ring me later then.'

'All right. Half seven?'

'Fine. I'll make a point of hanging on before going out tonight.'

Later, Katherine was so eager to start on the painted face she swallowed most of her salad lunch without tasting it. She worked with mounting anticipation, and felt a warm tide of relief flood through her as she identified unmistakable brush strokes. Lighter tones began to appear in the dark hair clubbed back from the face, and at last she gave a crow of pure triumph as a signature flash of light on a stray hair provided the last piece of the puzzle.

'Well?' she demanded, when James rang in response to her update.

'One of his minor early works, of course,' he said jubilantly, 'but even without seeing it in the flesh, I'm sure it's Gainsborough.'

She let out a deep heartfelt sigh. 'Hallelujah, so am I!'

'Of course you are. Have you told the client?'

'No. He's away for the day, so I'll break the glad news when he gets back.'

'Well done. And once you've done that, Katherine, there's no need for you to hang on there any longer,' he pointed out.

'No. No, there isn't,' she agreed quietly, feeling suddenly flat. 'Actually, James, unless it's going to cause problems at the gallery, I'd like to stay until my scheduled flight on Sunday. I fancy a day or two in the sun.'

'Fine by me. You finished the job sooner than I expected. Besides, Judith's finger is firmly on the pulse at the gallery.' He chuckled. 'I'm such an impossible patient she's glad to get away from me, poor darling.'

'Then hurry up and get well! Thanks, James. I'll let you know when the painting's on its way.'

Katherine closed her phone and sat staring at the face in the painting. She was pretty sure it hadn't turned up during past research, so why did he look so familiar? He was young. No more than twenty, at a guess. She jumped as Lidia rattled a tea tray behind her.

'You stop now, yes?'

Katherine nodded. 'I'm dying for some tea.'

Lidia put the tray on the other table and came to take a look. She shook her head in surprise. '*Engracado*—he look like Senhor Roberto.'

Katherine's eyes opened wide in sudden comprehension. 'Of course! You're right, Lidia. That's why he looks so familiar. I should have seen it before—the eyes and those eyebrows. Not the mouth so much, and the hair is straight, but there's definitely a resemblance. When will Senhor Sousa be home, do you think?'

'*Cinco horas*, maybe.' Lidia held up five fingers. 'Jorge telephone when they leave.'

'In that case I'll drink this tea, then have a bath. I'll take the painting upstairs with me.' Katherine smiled sheepishly. 'I want it to be a surprise.'

Lidia laughed. 'A very nice surprise!'

Katherine carried the painting upstairs later and laid it on the chest at the foot of the bed, too tired afterwards to risk staying long in the bath. She wrapped her wet hair in a towel so she could stretch out on the bed, and went straight to sleep.

She shot upright when her phone rang, rolling her eyes as she saw the time. 'Hi, Andrew,' she said, resigned.

'Do you know what time it is?' he said furiously. 'I'm due at a legal dinner tonight!'

'Then you'd better be on your way. Sorry. I've been working so hard I fell asleep after my bath.'

'For God's sake, how hard can it be, dabbing at a painting all day—?'

Katherine cut him off mid rant. Andrew had always claimed he found her work fascinating. Not any more, apparently. She got up quickly and, after a moment's hesitation, zipped herself into the green dress which did such good things for her shape. She brushed her hair into a shining bell and did her face, fastened gold studs in her ears, then switched on her phone again. No point in cutting herself off from the world just because Andrew was being a pain. It rang immediately, but this time her caller was Rachel Frears, her room mate at university and close friend ever since.

'What's up with Andrew?' Rachel demanded. 'He just rang me in a right old tizz. Says you hung up on him. Has he been a naughty boy? He even asked me to apologise for him.'

'That's new!' Andrew and Rachel had not taken to each other. 'He's annoyed because I took off to Portugal without him, and I've been working too hard since to ring him.'

'Does he demand regular phone sex, then?'

Katherine hooted. 'He'd be lucky! How's it going in the world of breaking news, Miss Hotshot?'

'I wish! I've just done a riveting features item on the ten hottest dress shapes for autumn. By the way, how come your work takes you to the beach, while mine keeps me here in an office?'

'I'm not at the beach. I'm in the Minho in the north.'

'So who's this man who's paying you to have a holiday, then?'

'Hey—I'm working my socks off!'

'Which doesn't answer my question, Dr Lister.'

'I'll give details when I get home—' Katherine broke off at a knock on the door. 'Got to go—dinnertime. I'll ring you before I leave.'

Katherine left Pascoa at the foot of the stairs and made for the veranda unescorted. The click of her heels on the polished stone floor brought Roberto into the hall to meet her, a look in his eyes which sent her pulse into overdrive.

'Good evening, Katherine. You look very beautiful.' So beautiful it was hard to remember that this goddess was the intellectual historian he'd found so daunting at their first meeting.

'Thank you,' she said, outwardly composed.

'How was your day?'

'Very busy.' She eyed him closely in the soft lighting on the veranda, but he looked no more tired than usual. 'How did you get on with your doctor?'

'He was pleased with my progress,' he said with satisfaction, and filled two wine glasses. 'And the *fisioterapia* was not such torture today.' He touched his glass to hers and smiled. 'Perhaps because your company this evening is my reward.'

Not sure how to answer that, Katherine sat in the chair he pulled out for her. 'I'm glad you had a good day. I did too.'

Roberto sat beside her, his eyes bright with anticipation. 'You have made progress?'

She nodded and jumped to her feet. 'I should have brought the painting down with me—I'll just run up and get it.'

Roberto got up more slowly. 'Please do not run, Katherine. Jorge is not here, and if you fall I cannot pick you up.'

And this, Katherine could tell, bothered him enormously. 'I'll just walk quickly,' she promised and hurried out into the hall.

Roberto followed and crossed to the foot of the stairs, watching as Katherine mounted them as though she had wings on her heels, the clinging fabric of her dress outlining her shape so exactly his mouth watered. His lips tightened. If she had finished work on the painting she would soon leave. He must find some way to persuade her to stay longer. He smiled as he saw her reappear, moving slowly now, as though she carried the Holy Grail. She descended the stairs with care, her eyes glowing over the canvas.

'Here he is. Shall we take him into the *sala* under the lights right away? Otherwise Lidia will be serving dinner.'

'*Sim senhora!*' Roberto limped rapidly across the hall to turn on the overhead lights in the *sala*. Katherine unveiled the canvas and put it on the desk, Roberto's indrawn breath as they leaned over it all the reward she needed.

'I've cleaned him up as much as I could,' she explained. 'Our top restorer will remove the stubborn bits with her scalpel. Then she'll make the necessary repairs and top the whole thing off by replicating—as near as possible—the original glaze finish. There's no signature, which was quite common, but James shares my opinion. Even from just the photograph I sent him he thinks there's no doubt about the artist.'

'Dare I guess?' he said huskily, his eyes glued to the canvas.

'Please do.'

Roberto took in a deep breath and turned to face her. 'Thomas Gainsborough?'

Katherine's radiant smile was all the answer he needed. He let out a shout of triumph and caught her in his arms and kissed her. His arms fell away at once and he stood back, a wry smile on his lips.

'I beg your pardon, Katherine.'

'No problem,' she assured him breathlessly. 'I could have kissed someone myself when James confirmed it.'

For a moment she thought Roberto would kiss her again, but he turned away to look at the picture.

'Lidia thinks he looks like you,' Katherine told him.

'*E verdade?*' He eyed the portrait in surprise. 'You agree with her?'

'I do now. At first I just thought he looked familiar, and couldn't think why. I was sure I'd never turned him up during my research, so it was only when Lidia commented on it that I saw the resemblance.'

Roberto smiled crookedly. 'He is much prettier than me.' He looked closely at the painted face. 'But he is familiar, *com certeza*. The first time I saw him I felt this, even disguised with such dark paint.' He shook his head. 'Come. We must return; Lidia will not be pleased if dinner is spoiled.'

Katherine hardly knew what she ate in her excitement, which Roberto shared, all vestiges of his normal melancholy gone as they discussed the painting.

'Will you keep it?' asked Katherine at one stage.

He shook his head. 'Now the provenance is confirmed I cannot hang it here because of security. Instead, I shall give our young man away as a very special Christmas present.'

'So your maiden will have to languish alone in the *sala*.'

'No, Katherine, she will be part of the same present. I will hang some other painting in the *sala*.'

Some present! Katherine hotly envied the lucky recipient, and looked up with a smile as Jorge came to clear away.

'Would the *senhora* like dessert?' he enquired.

Since the *senhora* had barely noticed the excellent fish she'd eaten, Katherine nodded, smiling. 'Yes, please.'

'You have not eaten dessert before,' observed Roberto when Jorge had gone.

'Tonight I'm in the mood to celebrate,' she told him, eyes sparkling.

Roberto looked at her in silence for a moment, his euphoria dimmed.

'What's the matter?' Katherine demanded. 'Are you in pain?'

He shook his head. 'I realise that now your work is done you will leave.'

There was a pause while Jorge appeared with a custard tart for Katherine, and then left them to a silence so intense it was tangible.

'Actually,' said Katherine, when she could bear it no longer, 'I'm not going home just yet. It was always my intention to go on to Viana do Castelo for a couple of days once my mission here was accomplished.'

Roberto's eyebrows rose. 'You are staying at a hotel there?'

'I'm not booked anywhere. I had no idea how long I'd be here at the Quinta. But if there was time afterwards I planned to ask for transport to Viana do Castelo and chance finding somewhere for the rest of my stay.'

'When is your flight?' he demanded.

'Sunday.'

He gave her the rare illuminating smile that lit up his entire face. 'Do you have a reason for staying in Viana?'

She shook her head. 'Only that it's not far from here, and from the guidebook it seemed like a pleasant place to recover. I've concentrated so hard on the painting I fancy a couple of days doing nothing but swim and sunbathe before getting back to the gallery.'

'But you could do those things here!' He leaned forward. 'Katherine, stay here at the Quinta until you fly home.'

She gazed at him in silence, her pulse racing.

'All I ask is your company, I swear.' He waited, but when she said nothing he slumped back in his chair. 'Forget I asked. Jorge shall drive you to Viana whenever you wish.'

She cleared her throat. 'Couldn't *you* drive me there tomorrow?'

His eyes narrowed. 'Why?'

'To ship the painting to James.'

'Unnecessary. A courier will collect it.'

'Pity.' Katherine smiled at him. 'I thought we might have lunch somewhere afterwards.'

Roberto's eyes narrowed. 'Is that a condition for your stay here?'

'No. Of course not.' She looked at him very directly. 'I thought it might do you good to get out for a while.'

'I do get out—to the hospital.' His smile was grim. 'I have faced danger many times in the past, but now I look like a monster I am not brave enough to eat in public, Katherine.'

'You look nothing like a monster,' she said flatly. 'But I understand how you feel.'

His eyes locked with hers. 'Then stay, Katherine.'

She looked at him in silence for a while and at last nodded, smiling wryly. 'Yes, I will. Though I'm not sure I should. Life will seem very humdrum back at home afterwards.'

'But you have a lover there.'

'Once and for all, Andrew is not my lover.' Her eyes flashed. 'And after the fuss he's made about my coming here, I'm not sure I even think of him as a friend any more.'

'Yet he wants you to live with him, no?'

'Because he thinks it's a sure way to get me to sleep with him,' she said; and regretted the words the moment they were out.

Roberto smiled broadly. 'Almost I pity this man. Because you will not do as he wishes, will you, Katherine?'

'No.' As she looked into Roberto's gleaming, heavily lashed eyes it was clear that the relationship Andrew wanted was never going to happen.

'He cannot be the first man eager to be your lover,' Roberto said, taking some cheese with sudden appetite.

'True. But there've been relatively few relationships in my life.'

Roberto eyed her questioningly. 'Why, Katherine?'

It was not a habit of hers to discuss her personal life, but he seemed genuinely interested in her so why not? Once she left Portugal she would never see him again. 'I need to like and respect a man before I get physically close to him. So when I was a student I was considered weird because I was selective, rather than a serial bed hopper.'

His eyes lit with laughter. 'The men you selected were greatly envied, no?'

'There weren't that many! I was just as happy with friends of my own sex, one of whom, Rachel Frears, is now engaged to Alastair, my tenant.' She sighed. 'They will naturally want to move somewhere else together, so I'll soon be looking for someone to replace him.'

'This is necessary for you, financially?'

Katherine nodded matter-of-factly. 'I love my job, but the salary isn't huge, and to keep my house I need the rent from the flats.' She ate some of the tart, eyeing him curiously. 'Did you enjoy life as a student?'

'I did not go to college.' He waited. 'You do not ask me why?'

She shook her head. 'I feel privileged to know the truth about your accident, Roberto, but you don't have to tell me anything else.'

'At last you say my name!' He leaned nearer to touch her hand. 'You must surely wonder how I live here, in luxury, yet do nothing that entitles me to such a life.'

She sat very still as his fleeting touch sent her pulse haywire. 'I assumed that your parents are wealthy enough to make that possible.'

'This is true,' he agreed. 'But until the accident I worked hard on the Estancia. Then I came here to a friend's wedding and met Elena, who almost killed me.' He smiled mirthlessly. 'Fate is a cruel mistress, *nao e*? For the time being I am no help to anyone. But I am striving to get fit as quickly as my body will allow and soon,' he added fiercely, 'I shall go back to Brazil and relieve my father of the work involved in running Estancia Grande. It is my heritage,' he added simply.

It was later, after Jorge had bidden them goodnight, before Katherine asked the question she'd wanted to ask the moment Roberto brought the subject up.

'The danger you faced in the past—was it anything to do with the work you did on the Estancia?'

'No, it was not.' He smiled sardonically. 'But I worried my mother greatly.' He paused, eyeing her closely. 'Are you tired, Katherine?'

'Not in the least. I had a nap earlier on, so sleep won't come easily tonight.'

'Then will you walk with me in the moonlight?'

'I'd love to,' she said eagerly, and got up, holding out her hand to him.

Roberto took it in his as he got to his feet. As they passed the pillar at the top of the veranda steps he flicked a switch, and lamps lit up throughout the gardens.

'How lovely,' she said, delighted. 'If you'll consent to take my arm, Senhor Sousa, you won't need your stick.'

'It will be my great pleasure,' he assured her as they set out on the beautifully kept paths. 'I come here alone at night when I cannot sleep. But it must surely annoy you to walk so slowly?'

She chuckled. 'I admit that it did when I wanted to get back to work, but tonight it's good just to stroll in the night air. I'm in no rush to get to bed.'

While Roberto, with Katherine's fragrance surrounding him, suddenly burned to pick her up and rush her to *his* bed. With no hope of achieving this, he schooled his clamouring libido and concentrated on the feel of her arm linked in his and the pleasure of the moment instead. It was some time since he had been in such close proximity with a woman. Not that the women he'd known in the past, other than his mother and his young wife, had ever walked further than from his car into some expensive restaurant.

'Why did you chuckle?' asked Katherine, looking up at the profile outlined by the moonlight.

'It is not polite to talk of women I've known in the past, but it occurred to me that none of them would have agreed to a walk in the dark—or even in daylight.'

'Were there very many?'

'Enough.' He shrugged. 'I had money to spend. And until the accident I was not bad to look at.'

A bit of an understatement, thought Katherine, resisting the urge to move closer. 'Were they all actresses like the lady who crashed your car?'

'There were also models.'

No surprise there. 'But how did you meet them? You said your Estancia was a long way from the nearest town.'

'I was many years working away from home before I returned to work on the Estancia.'

'You're very mysterious about what you did in those years away,' remarked Katherine.

'It was nothing criminal,' Roberto assured her, and smiled as she exclaimed in delight as they reached the pool.

'How lovely it looks in the moonlight!' She made for a wrought iron bench at the far end. 'Shall we sit for a moment to admire it?'

'You are tactful and think I need to rest, no?' he said as they sat down.

'Not at all. The rest is for me in these heels.' She leaned back with a sigh of contentment. 'Do you have a pool on the Estancia?'

'Yes. My father is enlarging it, ready for when I go home. As you say,' he added wryly, 'I have much to be thankful for—more than I deserve.' He turned to look at Katherine. 'When my mother agreed to leave me here to recover she did not know that fate would send you to me.'

She looked away. 'It was James who sent me, not fate.'

He laughed softly. 'I prefer my version.'

'You speak very good English, Roberto.'

He shrugged. 'It was necessary for me to learn. But I can do nothing about my accent.'

'Nor should you—it's very attractive.' So attractive it sent shivers down her spine.

'I am pleased you think so,' he said, in a tone which made the shivering worse. 'You are cold, Katherine. We must return to the house.'

She stumbled as she got up and Roberto leapt to steady her, but his leg gave way and they fell back on the bench in a tangled heap, laughing breathlessly. His arms tightened. 'I must let you go,' said Roberto with regret. 'If I do not you will run away tomorrow, no?'

CHAPTER FOUR

IF SHE had any sense she would! 'Probably,' Katherine said lightly, 'so let's walk back to the house.'

Roberto got to his feet at once and held out his hand. As they walked slowly back, she would have given much to surrender to instinct and melt into Roberto's arms for the kiss she had wanted just as much as he had. But one kiss would inevitably lead to more than that, and this time, with this man, her resistance was at an all-time low. He was right. It took very little time to fall in— what? Love or lust? Either way, it felt very dangerous in this moonlight.

When they reached the house Roberto bowed over her hand very formally in the hall.

'*Boa noite*, Katherine. *Dorme bem*.'

'Goodnight, Roberto. I hope you sleep well too.'

He gave a short, mirthless laugh. 'I doubt that.' He smiled suddenly. 'But if I lie awake I will take pleasure in thinking of the day I spend with you tomorrow.'

'No exercises?'

'I will finish early, and wait for my swim until you can join me. If you will?'

Katherine smiled up at him. 'I'll look forward to it.'

'I also.' He raised her hand to kiss it, and then

walked with her to the foot of the stairs. '*Ate amanha,* Katherine.'

She said goodnight and went up the stairs without looking back. She was in bed later, looking at the moonlight filtering through the slats of the blinds, before she remembered that Roberto had not explained the danger of his past life after all. She hesitated, cast a look at her laptop on the dressing table, and then gave way to temptation. She could find out right now. Something she could have done the moment she'd learned his first name, if she hadn't been so preoccupied with the painting. Katherine slid out of bed to switch on the laptop, and sat transfixed when her search led her to a shot of a younger unscarred Roberto. It was hard to tear her eyes from the handsome, laughing face to read the caption below.

Roberto Rocha Lima Tavares de Sousa, the racing driver professionally known as Roberto Rocha, was often compared during his budding career to his compatriot, Ayrton Senna, who died so tragically years previously on the Imola racetrack in Italy. But after only a few successful seasons, when the world championship seemed a probability rather than just a possibility in his future, Roberto Rocha retired from the track and returned home to Brazil.

Katherine's fascinated eyes stayed glued to the screen as she read about Roberto's progress from winning almost every race he entered as a youngster in his karting days, then went on to success at every stage on his way to the top. Her lips twitched when she found he'd made the headlines as much for his playboy lifestyle as for his prowess at the wheel of a racing car.

She stared at the laughing, handsome face for so long it was late when she switched off the machine and got back into bed. Hugh and Alastair were ardent fans, but her interests lay with rugby and tennis. Motorsport had never had the least appeal, though occasionally she'd read about its biggest stars in the papers; the slim young men in jumpsuits and helmets which gave them a Martian uniformity as they diced with danger to earn their spectacular money. She smiled wryly. With success in such a glamour sport, a parade of actresses and models had been inevitable for someone with Roberto's looks and money. Yet he'd given it all up to return to the Estancia. She wondered why. And, now she came to think of it, his interest in paintings seemed an odd combination with his past career. She would ask him about it tomorrow.

Katherine was ready in shorts and T-shirt over a jade one-piece swimsuit when her breakfast arrived, but felt too keyed up to eat much of it because the sun was shining outside, and Roberto might already be waiting for her. She ate half a roll, swallowed a cup of tea and, armed with a towel, managed to make it through the house unescorted for once. She sprinted through the gardens to the pool, where parasols were already open to shade the steamer chairs ranged alongside it. She shed her outer clothes, left them on the iron bench and lifted her face to the sun for a moment before diving neatly into the water. By the time she'd completed two lengths Roberto appeared, holding a pile of towels, and she hoisted herself out, smiling.

'Good morning.'

As she stood up his eyes lit with something which made her want to dive for cover.

'*Bom dia, sereia linda!*'

'I know *bom dia* is good morning,' she panted, wringing water from her braid. 'What was the rest of it?'

'It means beautiful mermaid, Katherine. How are you today?'

'Much better for my swim—aren't you coming in?'

'I will soon.' He handed her a couple of towels. 'Let us sit in the sun for a while first.'

Katherine wrapped herself in a large towel sarong fashion and mopped her face with another as she followed him to a deckchair. 'What a heavenly morning.'

Roberto eased himself down beside her. 'Did you sleep well?'

'Not that well.' She braced herself. 'In fact I have a confession to make. Last night, Roberto, I invaded your privacy. I looked you up on the Net.'

He shrugged, unperturbed. 'Such information is open to all who care to look, Katherine.' He raised an eyebrow. 'So. Now my past is the open book to you.'

'A very glamorous past!'

'It was not all glamour,' he assured her. 'To achieve success in motorsport, a driver must make sacrifices. I devoted many years of my life to it, and left home and family when I was young to do it.'

'That must have been hard!'

'It was. I missed my family and felt great *saudade* for my home.' He smiled reminiscently. 'But every time I got in the car and closed my helmet ready to race, it was the only place in the world I wanted to be.'

'Yet at the height of your success you gave it up and went home.'

'I had no choice, Katherine.' He let out an unsteady

breath. 'My older brother Luis was my father's right hand at the Estancia. Like me, he had ridden as soon as he could walk. But in a storm when he was out with the herd his horse was frightened by lightning and threw him. The fall would not have been fatal, but the horse's hoof struck my brother's head and killed him instantly.'

Katherine gazed at him in horror. 'Oh, Roberto, how tragic!'

Roberto nodded sombrely. 'I returned home immediately to support my parents in their grief, intending to stay for a while before returning to the track. I knew well it had been hard for them to let me follow my dream, constantly afraid that I would die on the track like Senna. Yet I had no serious accidents during all the years I was racing.' His mouth twisted. 'The only time I came near to death was driving from a restaurant.'

'But that was because your friend Elena was at the wheel,' Katherine pointed out.

'*E verdade*. But she was no friend of mine.'

'You don't speak to her now?'

His jaw clenched. 'She blames me for the loss of her career.'

'Because you couldn't lie for her?'

'*Exatamente*. She rang so often to say I had ruined her life I changed my phone. When she could not reach me she rang the number here at the Quinta, which was a big mistake because my mother answered.' He gave an evil chuckle. 'I don't know what *Mamae* said to her, but Elena has not contacted me since.'

'Did you care for her?'

'Not at all. I hardly knew her.' Roberto pushed his sunglasses into his hair to look into Katherine's eyes. 'At my friend's wedding Elena introduced herself to me to beg a great favour. She offered to pay for a meal if I would take her out in my car. Good PR, she told me. It would get her more screen time and therefore more money. I was amused by her honesty and agreed to drive her to the restaurant of her choice in my Maserati, but declined payment for my dinner. She had arranged for a photographer when we arrived, but fortunately he did not stay to witness our violent argument when we left.'

'An argument, even though you'd known her such a short time?'

'She offered sex in exchange for the large sum of money she was desperate for.' His mouth turned down in distaste as he put the glasses back on. 'She flew into a rage when I refused. The sum was nothing to me, she argued, but it would mean everything to her.'

'If she was in regular work in a television series, even in a minor role, surely she earned good money herself,' said Katherine, surprised.

'These are the words I said to her, but she refused to tell me why she needed such money. When I said no she snatched my keys out of my hand and ran for the car, screaming that now I *must* give her money to get it back.' His mouth twisted. 'I was a fool. I should have let her take it. But it was my beloved Maserati, you understand, so I wrenched open the door to dive into the passenger seat as she took off. She had no experience of such a powerful machine and failed to control it. I grabbed the wheel as we hit a bend but could not prevent the crash which ended all hope of returning to my career on the track.' He shrugged. 'My parents blame Elena, but she did not force me to get in the car. A man who values a piece of machinery more than his own safety has only himself to blame, *nao e*?'

Katherine was silent for a moment, eyeing him thoughtfully. 'She isn't hugely clever this lady, is she?'

He smiled. 'Why do you say that?'

'From what I read about you last night, she tried to sell you something women stand in line to give you for free,' she said bluntly.

He hunched a shoulder. 'If they did, they do so no longer.'

'Probably because you're hiding from them,' said Katherine practically. 'Come *on*, Roberto. Be positive. You've got a scar and a limp, but both of them will improve. You could have been killed but you're alive—' She bit her lip, flushing when Roberto gave a shout of laughter.

'It is good you did not choose a career in nursing!'

She grinned. 'I'd make a good Nurse Ratched in *One Flew over the Cuckoo's Nest*.'

He shook his head. 'You are not capable of such cruelty, Katherine.'

Her eyes dropped. 'I think I'll have another swim. Are you coming in?'

'*Pois e.*' He stood up to strip off his shirt and jeans. He held out his hand to her, but drew back, smiling wryly. 'It is best you get up unaided, or we have a repeat of last night, no? I would enjoy it, but you would not.'

'I wouldn't say that,' she said demurely, then ran along the side of the pool and dived in. When she turned at the end, laughing as she trod water, he was standing at the edge of the pool, shaking a finger at her. But he was laughing again, she saw with satisfaction, noting that lean though he might be, Roberto had the powerful legs of a man used to a life on horseback, plus a muscular torso for the same reason, or maybe as the result of the fitness regimes all racing drivers endured to stay at the top of their game. One look at that taut bronzed body and no woman in the world would care a toss about his facial scar. 'Come on in,' she called. 'The water's lovely.'

So are you, *linda flor*, thought Roberto as he dived in. He reached her in a few powerful strokes and exerted stern self control to keep from snatching her close as she smiled up at him. *Deus*, it had been too long since he held a woman in his arms.

'I won't challenge you to a race because I don't do much swimming these days,' she said with regret. 'But I'll try to keep up with you for a while.'

'We shall take it easy,' he promised, but after a couple of lengths she grinned at him and put on speed and he laughed, accelerating to keep up with her. But soon Katherine began to lag behind.

'I'm done,' she spluttered as he towed her to the steps.

'You swim well, Dr Lister.'

'But I'm seriously out of practice. You, on the other hand,' she gasped, 'are not even out of breath.'

'Because I am not out of practice,' he agreed, thrusting his wet curls back. 'But now I must do more lengths to complete my daily workout. When you go in tell Jorge we need coffee in half an hour, *por favor*.'

'Will do.' Katherine wrung the water out of her braid, wrapped herself in a towel and as she dried off stood watching Roberto power through the water before she went back to the house.

Katherine gave the request for coffee and ran upstairs to shower. As she hurried into jeans and a scarlet T-shirt, she reminded the niggling voice of caution in her head that all too soon she would be back in her normal everyday life which, satisfying though it was from a work point of view, and even from a social one, there was nothing in it to compare with this halcyon period spent with Roberto de Sousa in his beautiful house. She would be unlikely to make a discovery as exciting as the Gainsborough again, for a start. Even when her research did turn up something promising, James always took over from then on. This period at Quinta das Montanhas was a one-off experience in every way, and she would savour every fleeting moment of it.

Roberto was gazing out into the garden from his usual post at the veranda pillar when she rejoined him. Her espadrilles made no sound on the shining floor and he turned sharply as she reached him, smiling in approval.

'You were quick!'

'I suppose the women you know take more time— and effort—to get themselves together!'

He eyed her with appreciation as he led her to the table, where a coffee tray waited for them. 'You need no such effort, Katherine. Lidia says you ate no breakfast, so break your rules about *doces* and take some of her little cakes.'

'I will. I'd forgotten how hungry I get after swimming. And you don't have to diet to fit into a racing car any more.'

'It is one advantage,' he agreed dryly. 'Though it was not dieting in the usual sense. I merely kept to those foods which made me strongest for the task. Part of which was mental as well as physical.'

'Did you get depressed if you finished low down in the points?'

'It was not depression exactly, but...what is the word?' He thought for a moment, then snapped his

fingers. 'Obsession! Because tenths of a second quali-
fying time meant better start position on the grid.' He
shrugged philosophically. 'I have no such obsessions
now.'

'Except for believing that your scar makes you into
a monster,' she said before she could stop herself.

Roberto drank some of his coffee, eyeing her thoughtfully over the rim of his cup. 'You do not think this,
Katherine?'

'You know I don't. In fact—' She managed to stop
herself this time, and coloured at his look of intense
interest.

'In fact,' he prompted.

Oh, well, in for a penny. 'When I saw you at the pool
it was obvious that no woman who saw you without your
clothes would care a toss about the scar.'

He gave a delighted laugh, shaking his head as her
colour heightened. 'You are so good for me, Katherine
Lister. I thank you for the compliment. But surely you
noticed that one leg is not as straight as the other?'

'No, I didn't.' She drained her cup hastily.

'You are blushing again! I embarrass you so much,
Katherine? *Disculpeme*; it is not my intention.' He eyed
her objectively. 'Though you look most beautiful when
you blush.'

'And you exaggerate, Senhor Sousa!'

'Roberto, *por favor!* And I tell the truth, Katherine.
Yours is a beauty not only of looks but of brain.' He
grinned. 'A powerful combination!'

She laughed. 'You're in a good mood today.'

He leaned to take the cup she'd filled for him. 'I have
thought much about what you said yesterday. You say
the truth, Katherine. I have my family at home in Brazil,
also this beautiful house here in the Minho and, unlike

my beloved brother, I am alive, with good honest work waiting for me at the Estancia when I am fit. I should be thanking God for this, not complaining about the scar and my leg—' He looked up as Jorge came to say the *Patrao* was wanted on the telephone.

'The lady refused to give her name,' he added in apology.

Roberto's eyes narrowed. '*Com licenca*, Katherine.' He snatched up his stick and limped away quickly.

When Roberto returned to the veranda his eyes were dark with fury he masked quickly as Katherine looked at him in question.

'*Que descaramento!*' He tossed his stick away and sat down. 'You have the phrase talk of the devil, *nao e*? The mystery caller was the subject of our conversation, Katherine.' His eyes hardened. 'Elena Cabral rang to beg for money again.'

'Did she say why this time?'

'She says she owes money for gambling debts, and has been threatened with violence if she does not pay. She tried to soften me with tears and much sobbing.'

'You don't believe her?'

Roberto shrugged. 'She is experienced actress, Katherine. Tears are easy for her. When I refused she made threats, screamed she would make me sorry.' He squared his formidable shoulders. 'There is no further harm she can cause me so let us forget about Elena and think of pleasanter things. A courier is coming to pick up the painting this afternoon.'

'I'll pack it for you, if you trust me with it,' Katherine said promptly.

'*Pois e*—you're the expert!' He stretched cautiously in his chair. 'I have been thinking,' he went on.

'About the painting?'

'No. About you, Katherine. I asked you to stay here at the Quinta instead of in Viana do Castelo, but I am sure it must be boring for you.'

'It's been anything but boring this morning!' She waved a hand at the sunlit vista outside. 'And what hotel could possibly offer more than this!'

'The company of other guests, perhaps, also a beach, and shopping in the town.' His lips twitched. 'All women like shopping.'

Spare cash for shopping was in short supply, due to the unromantic need for plumbing repairs back home, so Katherine laughed and shook her head. 'This one can survive without it, I promise.' She paused. 'But I would like to see a little more of the Minho.'

'You would like Jorge to take you on a drive after lunch?'

He had to be joking! 'I hoped you would be kind enough to drive me yourself, Roberto Rocha,' she said challengingly. 'After all, you're supposed to be a good driver.'

To her relief, he threw back his head and laughed. 'I am not just good, I am brilliant. And I would be most delighted to take you out this afternoon.' He looked at his watch. 'I kept the crate for the painting, so if you would now help me pack it, Katherine, we have just enough time before we eat.'

She sealed the crate out on the veranda, taking great care to make the painting secure for its journey to England. 'Where it was probably painted some time between 1752 and 1759,' she told Roberto. 'Gainsborough was based in a town called Ipswich about then before going off to find fame and fortune in London.'

He smiled with deep satisfaction. 'It is so good to talk with someone who shares my interest in such things.

Except for my mother, all women I have known were bored with the subject.'

'You obviously spent time with the wrong women,' said Katherine, grinning—then bit her lip. 'Sorry. I forgot you'd been married.'

He shrugged. 'Mariana had no interest in art. She wanted a home and children and a husband who wanted those things, too. At that time I did not.'

'You must have been very young when you met?'

'Much too young to marry. But Mariana was very pretty and sweet and because I had to leave for Europe to race I married her only a few weeks after we met. She was expecting my child by the time I left. She went back to her family, but soon afterwards she lost the baby. Because I could not get home right away she turned to a childhood friend for consolation. In time, she divorced me and married him.' His mouth turned down. 'Mariana's treatment hurt my pride—though I did not lack attention from other women.'

'So I discovered during my research!'

'Ah, but I did not act on it while I was married,' he said virtuously.

Katherine eyed him curiously. 'I had a vague idea divorce wasn't legal in Brazil.'

'At one time it was not,' he agreed, 'but in the seventies the law was changed, and these days divorce is a very simple matter. I am speaking in legal terms, you understand. To the devout, like my parents, marriage is for life.' He shrugged. 'Their only consolation about my divorce was my freedom to marry again and give them the grandchildren they long for. Our family is unusual in our country. Now Luis is gone, I am the only child.'

She nodded sadly. 'I have no siblings either.'

He looked at her very directly. 'You would like children, Katherine?'

She put the finishing touches to the packing case and straightened. 'Yes. But I would need a husband to father these children first, and I've never met anyone I could imagine in the role. And I'll have to get a move on because I'm already twenty-eight,' she added.

'So old,' mocked Roberto. 'I am years more than that—'

'Which is totally different. A man can go on fathering children for decades longer than Mother Nature allows a woman to be a mother.' Katherine patted the crate. 'When is the courier coming to collect him?'

'Later this afternoon, but we need not wait. Jorge will be here to send our young man on his way.'

CHAPTER FIVE

KATHERINE ran back downstairs after lunch to find Jorge hovering in the hall, looking anxious.

'Senhor Roberto must not drive too far, *Doutora.*'

'I'll see that he doesn't,' promised Katherine. 'In fact, I could say I prefer you to drive us, if you think he's not up to it today.'

Jorge looked horrified. '*Nao, Doutora!* Say nothing, *por favor.* He has much pride, you understand.'

'I do, perfectly,' she said, and patted his arm. 'Don't worry. I'll make sure he doesn't overdo things.'

'*Muit' obrigado.*' He smiled apologetically. 'Lidia is anxious.'

So was Jorge, thought Katherine with sympathy. She went outside to wait, wondering what car Roberto drove now the Maserati was gone. It was a surprise to see Roberto at the wheel of a gleaming black Range Rover. She ran round to the passenger door, smiling as she hopped up onto the seat.

'I was expecting a sexy sports car,' she said, breathing in the scent of leather and new car.

'It *is* a sports car, Katherine. A Range Rover Sport with a V8 supercharged engine,' Roberto said with relish.

'Of course it is,' she said, laughing.

'You may laugh at me,' he said with dignity, 'but this model is also automatic, which is easier for me right now.'

'And it's wonderfully comfortable!' Katherine secured her seat belt and sat back with a sigh of pleasure. 'Right, let's hit the road.'

Instead of driving at top speed as she'd expected, Roberto took her on a leisurely journey along the River Lima, pointing out places of interest as they went. Although, as Katherine told him, everything she saw in this part of the world was interesting to her.

'It's so green. It's quite different from how I imagined it,' she told him as they passed hilly fields edged with stone and greenery on smallholdings where agriculture, Roberto informed her, was sometimes still carried on in the traditional way, with use of oxen rather than machinery.

'You think only of the Algarve, with the cliffs and sandy beaches and Mediterranean climate which make a holiday playground. Here in the Minho, life is different. Slower, some say backward, but I say peaceful and traditional. And it is green here because it rains a lot,' he added. 'We shall drive to Viana do Castelo, which has good shops. You will like it.'

'Because I'm a woman and can't possibly exist without shopping,' she teased, and Roberto laughed.

'As in most of Portugal, you will find good shoes there, and all women love shoes.'

Katherine was no exception. 'I would enjoy some window-shopping,' she admitted. 'But you wouldn't, so I'll pass.'

'I have the dark glasses, also the hat,' he pointed out, tilting his straw Stetson over his eyes. 'And with you at my side no one will look at me, so it is no problem.'

He peered at her over his sunglasses. 'I would like to window-shop with you, Katherine.'

'Then we will,' she said, smiling at him.

'If you permit this I can manage without my stick,' he said, and tucked her arm in his as they left the car later to stroll in the town. He glanced down at her as she sighed. 'You are not happy to do this?'

'Of course I am.'

'So why do you sigh?'

'Because I know perfectly well I should have gone home as soon as I'd finished work on the painting.'

'Yet you stayed when I asked. Because you pitied me?' he demanded abruptly.

'Certainly not,' she retorted, and felt him relax. 'I feel sympathy, not pity.' She smiled up at him, winning such a dazzling smile in response her heart contracted.

'As I have said before, you are good for me, Katherine.'

'You can repay me by acting as tour guide.'

'*Sempre as seus ordems,*' he said promptly, and gestured grandly with his free arm. 'Here we are in the Praca da Republica, with fountain constructed in 1553. You are attending, *Doutora*?'

'Hanging on every word!'

'*Muito bem.* The Praca is the hub of daily life here in Viana, where the historian may find many types of architecture to admire.'

'This one's full of admiration,' she assured him.

'I am most pleased to hear it. The Renaissance building at the far end, the *Misericórdia*, has magnificent—'
He stopped, frowning at the arcades supported by female figures. 'I do not have the word.'

'Caryatids,' supplied Katherine.

'*Obrigado, Doutora Historiadora.*'

'Good heavens, is that what I am?'

'Amongst other things, yes, Katherine.' He grinned down at her.

'Please carry on with the tour, Senhor Guide. Or are you getting tired?' she asked anxiously.

'With your arm in mine, how could I be tired?' He led her round the square, pointing out the Baroque living in harmony with the Manueline in the architecture styles of the mansions whose wealth, Roberto informed her, had been derived from trade with Brazil as well as the rest of Europe. 'Enough history,' he said abruptly. 'Now we look at shoes.'

Katherine laughed, only too happy to gaze at the tempting wares in the shop windows, but remained steadfast in her refusal to buy anything at all, even the pair of slender-heeled nude beauties which made her mouth water.

'You like those?' said Roberto.

'I'm just looking,' she said firmly, and turned away. 'And now, Senhor Sousa, it's time we went home, or Jorge will scold me for not looking after you.'

'First we buy the shoes.'

And, short of causing a disturbance in the Praca da Republica, Katherine had to accompany Roberto into the shop. A few minutes later they emerged with the sandals, which fitted so perfectly and looked so fabulous Katherine had decided to forget about plumbing for once and splurge. But there was a nasty moment when she found that Roberto had already paid for the new shoes while she was resuming her old ones.

'Tell me how much they were and I'll pay you when we get back,' she insisted outside, and then eyed him anxiously as his limp became more pronounced. 'You're tired. We should have stopped sooner. Do you need a rest before we go back?'

'*Nao, 'brigado*,' he snapped. 'Let us get back to the car.'

'Don't be afraid to lean on me,' she told him, and slid her arm more securely through his, dismayed that he was so offended.

Once they were in the car on the way back to the Quinta, Roberto obviously more comfortable seated at the wheel, Katherine returned to the subject of shoe payment.

'They are a gift,' he said flatly.

'I can't accept them,' she said, equally flatly.

'*Deus me livre*, they are not diamonds,' he growled, and stared straight ahead in smouldering silence for the rest of the journey.

'Roberto, please try to understand,' she said miserably as they turned in at the gates of the Quinta. 'You've already paid handsomely for my services—' Damn, that came out all wrong. 'I mean—'

'I have enough English to know what you mean,' he snapped, and drove up the sweeping curves of the drive at breakneck speed to bring the car to a stop with panache at the great main door. 'If you cannot bring yourself to accept such a trifling gift from me, *nao importa*—throw them away.'

Before Katherine could reply, Jorge came hurrying to open the car door to help her out, and Roberto drove away round the house at a speed which left Jorge staring after him in consternation.

'He is in pain, *Doutora*?' he asked anxiously.

'Probably.' Also angry. Roberto Rocha de Sousa, it was plain, didn't take kindly to opposition.

'You would like tea?' asked Jorge as they crossed the hall.

Not if it meant an awkward encounter on the veranda while she drank it. Katherine smiled at him. 'I thought I'd just go up to my room for a while.'

'Tea will be brought to you,' he said firmly.

'Was the painting collected?'

'*Sim, senhora.* It is on its way to London.'

As she should be, too. Katherine sighed, feeling depressed after her altercation with Roberto. Dinner wouldn't be much fun tonight.

Lidia brought the tea up, which added guilt to Katherine's gloom.

'I should have had this downstairs and saved you the trouble,' she told the woman in remorse.

'Is no trouble,' said Lidia, surprised. 'I come myself because it is Pascoa's day off. You have nice trip?'

'Yes, indeed. I liked Viana do Castelo very much.'

'*Muito bem.* Now you have rest before dinner.'

Which was more than Lidia was likely to get without Pascoa's help. Katherine drank her tea, but concentration on her book proved so difficult she had a long shower instead, and afterwards spent more time than usual on her hair and make-up to boost her morale.

When Lidia arrived at dinnertime to announce that Senhor Roberto waited on the veranda she handed over the smart carrier bag containing the shoes. 'Senhor Roberto say you left this in car.'

Katherine went downstairs with considerable reluctance, wishing she could have eaten in her room. Which was stupid. She would have to face Roberto some time.

He came to meet her in the hall, a wry twist to his lips

when he saw she was wearing the shoes. '*Desculpe-me*, Katherine. I lost my temper.'

'I noticed!' She smiled. 'Are we friends again now?'

'Of course.' He ushered her out onto the softly lit veranda, filled two wine glasses and took the chair opposite, eyeing her challengingly. 'I thought perhaps you would not dine with me tonight.'

'No danger of that,' she assured him.

'Because you forgave my bad temper?'

She shook her head, grinning. 'Because I'm hungry.'

He grinned back, looking suddenly younger. 'You tease me! And I like it very much.' He sobered. 'I shall miss you so much when you leave, Katherine.'

'Won't you be going home to Brazil soon?' She smiled as Jorge appeared with a dish of *bolinhas*. 'Yummy! I love these.'

Roberto laughed. 'It is good to see a woman eat with such appetite.'

'I suppose the ladies in your past all existed on carrot sticks and fresh air!'

'It is possible they did in my absence,' he said cynically, 'but in my company they chose the most expensive dishes on the menu.'

'How did they get on with Lidia's cooking?'

Roberto shook his head. 'None of them came here. The Quinta is my retreat. I kept an *apartamento* in Lisboa while racing in Europe, and the rest of the season I was competing too far away to think of anything but the next race. I have always had complaints from women, starting with Mariana, that my concentration on my sport was so intense I had no emotion to spare for relationships.'

'You miss racing?'

'Very much. But as you told me, Doctor, I have much

to be grateful for. Including,' he added, as Jorge came in with a tray, 'Lidia's wonderful cooking.'

'Amen to that,' said Katherine reverently.

They kept to less emotive subjects over the meal, Katherine gratified by Roberto's interest in her work at the gallery. They were so absorbed in her account of one of James's major discoveries they looked up in consternation when Jorge rushed in looking worried and, with a word of apology to Katherine, spoke to Roberto in Portuguese as he handed him a letter.

Roberto studied it, his face grim. 'Jorge found this taped outside one of the *sala* windows,' he told Katherine. 'He did not find it until now when he was checking that all was secure for the night, as usual. I must look for myself; I will not be long.'

As he hurried off with Jorge, Katherine collected the dishes and carried the tray across the hall to the kitchen.

Lidia relieved her of it in dismay. '*Doutora*—I take that.'

'Jorge was busy with Senhor Roberto, so I made myself useful. May I look round?'

'*Pois é.*'

Katherine followed her into a large kitchen with state-of-the-art appliances living in harmony with an old cooking range which had obviously been left in place for its aesthetic qualities. 'What a marvellous room,' she exclaimed, and Lidia did her best to smile as she loaded the dishwasher.

'I feel much guilt because letter came when Jorge take me shopping.'

'It wasn't your fault,' soothed Katherine, and gave Lidia something to keep her busy. 'Could I possibly have some tea—and coffee for Senhor Roberto?'

The woman instantly sprang into action, then exclaimed in dismay as she loaded the tray. 'I did not serve *sobremesa*. I made *pudim de arroz*—rice pudding.'

'We'll have it later.'

Katherine took one look at Roberto's face when he rejoined her, and poured coffee for him. 'Did you find anything else?"

'No.' He discarded his stick and sat down, accepting the coffee gratefully. He showed her the note, which was written in large printed capitals. 'It threatens harm to me, my house and all who live in it if I do not pay the money.'

Katherine frowned. 'The person who delivered it must have seen Jorge and Lidia leave to go shopping. You think Elena is involved?'

He shrugged. 'I hope that no one else is after my blood.' He drained the coffee and stood up as the bell rang. 'It will be the *Guarda Nacional*. I rang them to report this.'

CHAPTER SIX

KATHERINE waited uneasily as Roberto went into the hall, wishing she could understand the rapid interchange as he made his report to the police. The wait seemed endless before she heard goodnights exchanged and the bolts rammed home on the great main door.

When Roberto rejoined her he apologised for the long wait. 'They wished to question Lidia and Jorge, also to inspect the *sala* and the window where the note was left. They have taken the note with them.' He sighed wearily. 'I need a drink. Join me in a brandy, Katherine. We must talk. Will you be too cold on the *varanda*?'

'Not at all.' She felt depressed. In the circumstances, she'd have to leave right away to save additional worry for Roberto by staying.

He poured brandy into glasses and handed her one. 'We both need this, I think.'

Katherine took a fiery sip and put the glass down. 'A good thing my flight is on Sunday, Roberto.'

'I know this,' he said grimly and drained his glass, shuddering as the fiery spirit hit its target. 'But do not be frightened, Katherine. I will not allow harm to come to you.'

'I'm not frightened for myself—at least, not much,' she added honestly. 'I'm more worried for you, Roberto.'

He glared at her. 'Because I am crippled and cannot defend myself?'

'For heaven's sake, cut the drama, Roberto, this is serious,' said Katherine impatiently and then bit her lip, eyeing him warily as he gave her a wry smile.

'*Desculpe-me*, Katherine. What are you trying to tell me?'

'The truth, Roberto.' She held his eyes. 'You're *not* physically capable of fighting off an attacker right now.'

He shook his head in scowling amazement. 'We have so little violent crime here I cannot believe this.'

'I find it hard to believe myself, but it's only sensible to take precautions.'

'You are right, *sem duvida*.' Roberto glanced out into the night. 'And to start such precautions, it is best we go inside. I shall turn off the lights here and lock the doors then take you upstairs.'

'You don't have to do that—'

He eyed her impatiently. 'Of course I do, Katherine. No one else sleeps on the upper floor. I will not rest until I know you are safe inside your room.'

Secretly very grateful for his escort, she waited while he locked up and then offered her arm for support.

Roberto gladly abandoned his walking stick for the slow ascent, but in such close, tempting proximity to her body he felt himself harden in fierce response. He clenched his teeth against the force of it, telling himself he would take her only as far as her room. His mouth tightened. But then she would be totally alone up here should the unthinkable happen and some *meliante* break in.

Katherine slid her arm from his and took his hand

as they reached the landing. 'What's troubling you, Roberto?'

Many things, he thought savagely, not least the desire to seize her in his arms and kiss her senseless. 'I worry because you will be alone up here tonight.'

'I've been alone up here every night since I arrived,' she pointed out.

'But until today you were in no danger—'

'You surely don't think someone would actually try to break in?' Katherine stared at him in consternation.

He thrust a hand through his hair, his eyes bitter. 'Yesterday, I would have laughed at such an idea. Tonight, who knows? I cannot endure the thought of you alone and vulnerable, so far away from me.'

Katherine wasn't very happy about it, either. Even if by some miracle she managed to sleep, the mere possibility that someone might try to climb in through her window would give her nightmares. She opened her bedroom door and crossed to the bedside table to switch on a lamp. 'Could you lock the windows, please? As one of those precautions, I'll keep them closed tonight.'

He shut the door behind him and crossed the room to secure the tall windows, his eyes raking the moonlit gardens. 'Do not worry, Katherine. It is bright as day outside. Only a fool would try to get in on a night like this.'

'I hope you're right,' she said doubtfully.

'You are afraid?'

'A bit.' She hesitated. 'Are you tired, or could you stay and talk for a while?'

Roberto turned to face her. 'I am not tired, but I will not stay.'

Katherine gave up. 'Goodnight, then.'

Roberto closed his eyes in desperation, and then

opened them again, abandoning all effort to hide the hunger in his eyes. 'If I stay I will want more than just to talk. And I promised to keep you safe, *nao e*? That must mean safe from me, also.'

She moved closer, meeting the look head on. 'Stay, just the same. Please?'

Roberto gave a despairing groan and seized her in his arms, his lips devouring hers in a kiss which went on so long they were both shaking when he raised his head at last to look into her dazed eyes.

'You see?' he said through his teeth. 'One kiss and we set the world on fire.' His eyes burned into hers. 'I am entranced by your mind and your knowledge of art, *e verdade*, but also by your beautiful body, Katherine.'

'I am by yours, too, Roberto,' she said candidly, her colour rising.

He swallowed convulsively. 'You mean that?'

'Every word.'

He let out a deep, ragged sigh and drew her down beside him on the bed. '*Deus*, I thought no woman would ever look at me with pleasure again.'

Katherine leaned against him, exulting in the rapid thud of his heartbeat against hers as she breathed in the scent of his heated skin. 'In the past you were accustomed to a great many women looking at you with pleasure?'

'Yes,' he said simply. 'Pretty playmates were part of the life I led after Mariana divorced me.' He raised her hand and pressed a lingering kiss in her palm. 'And you have no wish for marriage either, *nao e*?'

She shook her head. 'Not true. I just haven't met a man I want for a husband.' Nor even for a lover in the true meaning of the word. Until now.

He caught her by the chin and looked deep into her eyes. '*Agora*, Katherine, tell me you want me.'

'Of course I want you. I asked you to stay!'

'Because you are frightened.'

'And because I want you to make love to me, Roberto. Are you going to, or are you just going to talk about it?' She scowled at him crossly. 'I won't ask again!'

'You need not!' He kissed her in passionate assurance as they fell back on the bed together, the seduction of his seeking, smoothing hands so ravishing they took Katherine's breath away.

'*Eu te quero, amada,*' he whispered, his breath burning her skin.

No translation was necessary. Roberto's words sent such heat flaming through her Katherine pressed even closer to him, which only made the heat worse—or better. She would be gone soon and if she sent him away now she would regret it for the rest of her life. To make this clear, she kissed him in such explicit invitation he growled in delight against her parted lips, his hands caressing her to such a pitch of longing she helped feverishly when he undressed them both with urgent hands. She tensed as Roberto laid her on her back but, instead of immediately crushing her body with his, as she expected, he propped himself on an elbow and lay there just looking at her, his eyes moving over every inch of her as though he wanted to eat her up. She moved restively, unable to lie still under the glittering, hungry gaze.

'No. Do not move. For a little while just let me look at you, Katherine,' he said huskily. 'I want a picture of you in my mind, so that I can look back on this moment and remember.'

To her embarrassment, her nipples hardened in

response to his words, and he drew in a sharp breath and bent his head to tease and torment them with wickedly skilful lips and grazing teeth, while his hands made love to every curve and hollow of her responsive body. When they moved lower at last, his skilled, seeking caresses brought her up off the bed; her hands urgent on his back and, with a deep, relishing sigh, he slid over her. Her mouth dried as their bodies came into full, naked contact, the rasp of hair-roughened muscular thighs between the smoothness of hers so erotic her heart hammered in her chest.

'You told me,' he reminded her in a tone that made her breath catch, 'that you allowed such closeness only if you had feelings for the man. Do you have such feelings for me, Katherine?'

As if she was going to say no in this situation! She nodded wordlessly.

He gave her a glorious smile and kissed her mouth as he entered her body with a smooth, slow thrust which stunned them both by the sheer tactile pleasure of it until Roberto surrendered to the urging of his body and began to move, his lovemaking enhanced by the words he whispered in her ear until he had no more breath for talking as their bodies surged together in urgent rhythm that blotted out everything other than the pleasure they were giving each other, a frenzied joy so intense it was almost pain as completion finally engulfed them in a throbbing wave of rapture so intense it brought tears to Katherine's eyes.

Roberto held her tightly, his face buried in her hair. When he raised his head at last he frowned as he saw her tears. 'You are crying, *amada*?'

She shook her head, blinking the moisture from her

lashes. 'Just tears of wonder. I've never experienced anything so...so overwhelming before.'

His eyes gleamed with such blatant male satisfaction Katherine laughed as he kissed her tears away.

'Why are you laughing at me?' he demanded, raising his head.

'You looked so smug!'

'What is smug?'

How was she supposed to search for vocabulary in these circumstances! 'Pleased with yourself.'

'What man would not be pleased when his woman finds joy in his arms?'

His woman. Katherine thought that over with disquiet. 'Roberto—'

'Do not ask me to move, *querida*—unless I am crushing you?'

Now the subject had come up, she had to admit that he was, a bit. The lean, graceful body was surprisingly heavy. 'I was going to remind you about my flight.'

Roberto groaned, his arms tightening like steel bands. When she protested he rolled over, taking her with him to lie on top of him. He smiled up into her eyes, smoothing the hair back from her face. 'Better, *nao e*?' He pulled the sheet up to cover her and brought her head down to fit into his shoulder. 'Stay, Katherine,' he said, and kissed her. 'We have hours of tonight to enjoy together before we must part.'

Dawn came too soon for Katherine next morning. But her first thought as Roberto kissed her into warm, throbbing life again was the threat he received yesterday.

'What troubles you, *querida*?' he demanded. 'You do not want to make love again?'

Incredibly, she found she did, which astounded her

after the night they'd just spent together. He kissed and caressed her into such rapid response she postponed discussion of the problem until she could think and function again normally.

At last Roberto slid reluctantly out of bed. 'I wish we could shower together, but until my leg recovers this is not possible. It will be something to look forward to in future,' he whispered, and leaned to kiss her. 'While I take my lonely shower hurry through yours, Katherine,' he ordered, and began pulling on his clothes. 'Join me for breakfast on the varanda today. I am hungry.'

'So am I,' she admitted.

Roberto gave her a grin which brought such quick colour to her face he bent to kiss her pink cheeks. 'You are so beautiful when you blush. Be quick, *por favor.*'

'How about your exercises?'

He laughed. 'After such joyous exercise last night I will take a holiday from the painful kind today. So hurry.'

When Katherine joined Roberto the look on his face rang alarm bells. 'What's wrong?'

'There was an intruder here last night. An attempt was made to force the door to my part of the house. It was unsuccessful because I recently installed a new security system. Jorge checked all the outer doors, but he found nothing else.' He smiled into her worried eyes. 'They could not attack me because I did not spend the night in my room, *nao e*?'

'Thank God you didn't!' She bit her lip. 'Did Jorge wonder where you were?'

'I told him I slept in one of the rooms upstairs to ensure your safety.' He grinned. 'I did not say which one.'

She grinned back, but quickly sobered. 'I was right, Roberto. You're in danger from someone, Elena or not.'

'*E possiviel*,' he agreed reluctantly. 'I have informed the *Guarda*.'

'Good,' she said fervently, and smiled as Jorge appeared with a tray. 'Good morning.'

'*Bom dia.* Senhor Roberto says you also leave tomorrow, *Doutora*.'

'If possible, yes.'

He looked relieved and cast a look at his employer. 'Senhor Roberto should leave, also—'

'I am hungry, Jorge,' said Roberto gently. 'Perhaps you will leave us to enjoy our breakfast? We will leave discussion until later.'

'*Pois e*,' said the man, and hastily withdrew.

Katherine raised a disapproving eyebrow. 'You were a bit short with him, Roberto. The poor man is obviously worried about you.'

'I know he is. But I am eager to enjoy every moment of our first breakfast together, *carinha*.' He raised her hand to his lips.

But knowing it would also be their last, Katherine found it hard to enjoy the food, famished though she was. A direct result, apparently, of spending most of the night making love. A first in every possible way.

'What are you thinking?' asked Roberto.

She coloured slightly. 'I never realised how hungry one gets after a night of...of...'

'Love?' He grinned. 'It is plain you have not had the right lover until now.'

Wasn't that the truth! 'While we're on the subject, Roberto,' she said, pouring coffee for him, 'what happened last night was not...not usual for me.'

CATHERINE GEORGE   97

'Or for me,' he assured her, a look in his eyes that curled her toes. 'I have never experienced such rapture before.'

She gave him a wry smile as she filled her teacup. 'I bet you say that to all the girls, Roberto Rocha.'

His eyes flashed coldly. 'You are wrong, Katherine. I do not.'

'Then I apologise. I just want you to know that one-night stands are not a habit of mine.'

With intense concentration, he slit open a roll and filled it with ham. 'You think,' he said slowly, 'that I will think less of you because you made love with me last night?'

'It crossed my mind,' she admitted. 'Could you do one of those for me, please?'

He smiled. 'You may have this one. I will do another.'

'Thank you.' She munched on the roll for a while, thinking hard. 'What I'm trying to make clear is that last night was wonderful, unique, and totally outside my experience. But will never happen again.'

'*Por que*? I was not a good enough lover?' he demanded.

Katherine glared at him. 'Typical male reaction!'

'What else? I am a man, also *Brasileiro*—and *Gaucho*. I demand to know why we cannot repeat such pleasure, Katherine.' Roberto fixed her with a look which turned her heart over, then looked up impatiently as Jorge hurried onto the veranda.

'*Telefone*, Senhor Roberto. Dona Teresa.'

'My mother at this hour?' Roberto grabbed his stick and got up. '*Com licenca*, Katherine. Please eat more.'

She watched him hurry away, stick tapping. 'How is Lidia this morning?' she asked Jorge.

'She feels bad that we were out when the letter was delivered.'

'Far better you were both out than either of you got hurt, Jorge.'

He smiled gratefully. 'It is wise that you leave tomorrow, but it has been a pleasure to meet you, *Doutora*. Perhaps you will return soon.'

Katherine smiled non-committally, and with a bow Jorge took away the tea and coffee pots to replenish them. She wandered over to one of the pillars to gaze out over the garden, so lost in thought she was startled when Roberto's arms slid round her.

'You look sad, *carinha*,' he whispered in her ear.

She turned, smiling valiantly. 'Only because I'm leaving soon. But I'm glad you're leaving too.'

He smiled exultantly. 'We shall leave together. But not on a flight to England.'

Katherine tipped her head back to look up into his face. 'What do you mean?'

'I was a long time on the telephone, not only because my mother wished to talk. She had a sudden desire to know all was well with me.' He smiled. 'When I told her about our adventures she called my father to the phone. He said that I must leave at once. He is a very practical man, and suggested a most simple solution to this threat. I close the house, hire a security firm to guard it for a week or two, and give Lidia and Jorge a holiday.' He kissed her hard. 'And here is the best part. My parents invite you to accompany me to the Estancia, Katherine. So we are leaving from Lisbon tomorrow. After much telephoning, I have found two cancellations for a flight to Porto Alegre.'

Katherine stared at him aghast. 'But I've got to

get back to work—I can't just take off for Brazil, Roberto!'

His arms tightened. 'Why not? I will pay for more of your time, and Senhor Massey will give you leave.'

She pulled away, shaking her head vehemently. 'You can't just pay for me, Roberto. Money doesn't solve everything.'

'In this case it can buy me more time with you,' he said flatly. 'Come with me. Just for two weeks if that is all you wish, Katherine, to make up for the stress these threats are causing you.'

'It's not your fault, Roberto!'

'Of course it is my fault! When my friend returned from honeymoon he told me that Elena had been what you call a gatecrasher at his wedding. She got in with the photographer.' He shrugged. 'She saw me there and thought I would be an easy...mark is right?'

Katherine nodded.

'And I was,' he said bitterly. 'No one forced me to get in the car with her, so I know well I am responsible for what happened to me, but not for the loss of her TV job. Yet now she is beginning her *bobagem* over money again.'

Katherine shivered. 'It's such a good thing you're off to Brazil. You're out of her reach there.'

Roberto's eyes glittered hotly. 'But now things are changed between us, Katherine, I do not want to let you go. So come with me to the Estancia, *querida*.'

She shook her head sadly. 'I really can't do that, Roberto.'

His dark eyes locked with hers, willing her to say yes. 'Two weeks is all I ask, Katherine—for now.'

She pulled out of his grasp and turned away to look out over the garden. A fortnight in Brazil was a tempting idea. She had taken very little in the way of holidays lately. James was probably fit enough to take over the reins again by now, and his wonderful Judith would help out. An opportunity like this would never happen again in her lifetime. Her mouth tightened. Nor could she let it happen now. It had been against every principle she possessed just to let him pay for the shoes, so a fortnight's holiday in Brazil at his expense was right out of the question. And even if she were mad enough to give in to him it would be hell afterwards to fit into her normal way of life again. A life without Roberto Rocha Lima Tavares de Sousa.

The period before Katherine left the Quinta das Montanhas was dominated by constant persuasion from Roberto, who never let up with his demand that she fly to Brazil with him even though she was equally immovable with her refusal.

The plan to close up the house was carried out with military precision. As soon as the security firm had set up its base at the Quinta the following morning, Lidia's brother would arrive to take her with Pascoa to stay at his house in Braga. Jorge would then drive Roberto and Katherine to Porto for her flight to the UK, and afterwards take Roberto to Lisbon for his flight to Porto Alegre. During that eventful last day, while Roberto was involved with the cancellation of his medical and physio appointments, and giving notice of his intention to the *Guarda Nacional*, Katherine spent time on her own phone, informing those who needed to know that she was returning as scheduled.

When Katherine reported to James that she would be back in work on Monday she asked him about the Gainsborough. 'How does it look now, boss?'

'Nearly finished and looking good. It would arouse huge interest at auction, but de Sousa is adamant that I just ship it off to Brazil when it's ready.' He paused. 'Katherine, take a day off to recover and start on Tuesday. You sound tired.'

Due to sleep deprivation, amongst other things. 'It's been an eventful few days here.'

'Was the client a problem? I was a bit worried once I looked him up. Did you know he's actually Roberto Rocha, one-time glamour boy of the racing car circuit?'

'Not until I looked him up. Why were you worried?'

'Judith saw the shot of the chap in his glory days on my computer. My unimpressionable wife was bowled over.'

'Well, I wasn't,' she lied. 'See you Monday.'

CHAPTER SEVEN

ROBERTO elected to occupy the room next to hers that night instead of sharing her bed again, but after Katherine had tossed and turned for an hour her door opened and closed again softly and Roberto slid into bed with her, his naked body hot and hard against hers.

'I could not sleep,' he whispered.

'Neither could I.'

'I lay awake, wanting you very badly, Katherine.'

Since she had been doing the same, she responded with passionate fervour to his kisses as he slid her beneath him.

'I have been longing for this—for you—for a whole hour,' he said against her parted lips. 'I can wait no longer, *amada*.'

Neither could Katherine. No foreplay was required or necessary. Her body had been ready for him the moment it came into contact with his, and she gave a visceral little groan of satisfaction as he thrust home into her tight, welcoming warmth. The sorcery of her clenching inner muscles incited him to a wildness which left her revelling in the surprise of her own power, then regretting it when culmination left them shaking in each other's arms all too soon, stunned by the force of it.

'*Desculpe-me, querida,*' Roberto panted, raising his head a fraction. 'I was too fast.'

She shook her head vehemently. 'Tonight I wanted fast.'

'Our loving will always be fast when you caress me in such a way!'

She smiled up at him jubilantly. 'Never knew I could do that!'

He chuckled and kissed her nose, then turned her in his arms. 'Perhaps now we can both get some rest.'

Dazed by the force of their lovemaking, Katherine slept heavily in the warmth and security of Roberto's arms and woke early and heavy-eyed in the morning.

Roberto, however, looked annoyingly chipper. '*Bom dia, linda flor.*'

She shuddered, feeling nothing remotely like a beautiful flower. 'Are you always this cheerful in the mornings?'

'No. But how could I not be happy after last night?' His arms tightened, his eyes bright with sudden demand. 'Now you will change your mind, Katherine, *nao e*? You will come with me today.'

She eyed him suspiciously. 'Is that why you stole into my bed last night? To change my mind?'

He shook his tousled head. 'I came because I could not exist another moment without you.' He gave her a kiss so soft and sweet she wanted to cry. 'Hurry through your bath. We shall breakfast together before the security people arrive.'

Lidia arrived with tea while Katherine was dressing. 'I cook hot meal today,' she said in a tone that brooked no argument. '*Dez minutos,*' she added, holding up her hand twice.

'Thank you, Lidia.' Katherine smiled warmly. 'Are you happy about staying in Braga for a while?'

'It make Senhor Roberto happy, so I am happy,' said the woman simply. 'I help pack?'

'Almost done, thanks. I won't be long.'

Ready for travel in the black trousers and white shirt of their first meeting, Katherine hurried down to join Roberto.

'Ah!' he said with appreciation as he drew out her chair. 'Last night you were temptation in my arms, this morning you are severe *Doutora* again. I like this look, it is very sexy!' He sniffed the air as Jorge brought their breakfast. 'Lidia has made a hot meal this morning. She goes to Braga after you eat?'

'Her brother comes at eight,' Jorge informed him, and took the covers from the dishes. 'Lidia says please to eat everything.'

Katherine was only too happy to. Who knew when she'd be eating another meal? Up to date she'd never managed to eat much on a plane. At the mere thought of leaving Roberto to fly in the opposite direction, her heart contracted. 'Is yours a non-stop flight?'

He shook his head. 'There is a brief stop in Paris, then a longer one in São Paulo, where I must change to Congonhas Airport for the rest of the journey to Porto Alegre. There I board a smaller plane to reach the Estancia.'

She eyed him with sympathy. 'That's a very long time for you to stay immobile. How far is the road journey to Lisbon?'

Roberto moved his chair nearer and took her hand. 'Two hundred and forty or so of your British miles.'

'It's a lot of driving for Jorge today, too,' she said anxiously.

'He will have a break at Porto, since you insist on leaving me there. Afterwards, if I can persuade him, I will drive to Lisbon. You are thoughtful, Katherine Lister, but do not worry. Jorge enjoys driving as much as I do.' His eyes shadowed. 'Or I used to.'

'And still do, Roberto! The minute you're behind the wheel of your car you're a happy man.'

He smiled. 'You are right. I would drive all the way today from choice, but it would not be wise before a long flight.'

Katherine winced. 'When you get home, what will you do about your physio and exercises?'

'The pool is ready, and I know the exercises—*Deus*, how well I know them! I shall continue with them when I get to Estancia Grande.'

Knowing how constricted she felt on a plane with two legs in good working order, Katherine eyed him anxiously. 'How will you manage with your leg during the flight?'

'In first class, I will have room to stretch out.' He smiled. 'And I will be so brave the attendants will pay much attention to me.'

She could just imagine it, and busied herself with filling cups to hide a pang of jealousy.

'If you were with me,' he said softly, 'I would not mind the pain. Change your mind, Katherine. Come with me.'

'I can't!' She mopped quickly at a stray tear as Lidia came to say goodbye.

She gave Katherine a sharp look. 'You are sad to leave, *Doutora*?'

'I am indeed.' Katherine got up and kissed the woman's cheek. 'You've been so kind.'

Lidia smiled shyly and squeezed her hand. '*O prazer*

e meu, Doutora. Come back soon. My brother waits, and Pascoa is in the car, so I go now. Adeus.'

'She said the pleasure was all hers, Katherine,' said Roberto after he returned from seeing Lidia off. 'She says you must come back for another holiday one day.'

'I came to work, not for a holiday,' she reminded him.

He nodded in satisfaction. 'And I am most grateful to Mr Massey for sending you to me.'

'You weren't very pleased about it when you first saw me!'

'*E verdade*. You looked so daunting in your severe clothes and spectacles,' he demanded, taking her hand.

'Normally, I only wear those for computer work, but I thought they might impress you with my competence.' She smiled. 'Did it work?'

'*Sim, senhora*. It worked perfectly.'

'You weren't very friendly.'

Roberto looked her in the eye. 'I had no wish for a woman in my house while I look like this.'

Katherine leaned forward and planted a series of little kisses along the ridged flesh of his scar, and received a series of kisses on her mouth as response.

'You soon changed your mind,' she pointed out when she could speak.

His eyes gleamed. 'I was seduced by your intelligence!'

'Were you indeed?' she said wryly.

He raised her hand to his lips, his eyes suddenly very serious. 'So change that informed mind of yours, Katherine. Come to Brazil with me.'

This wasn't fair, she thought in despair. Roberto was making it harder by the minute to say goodbye to him.

It was almost a relief when the doorbell clanged and he went to speak to the head of the security firm.

While he was gone, Katherine took a wistful look over the gardens, then went upstairs to get her belongings together. She checked she'd left nothing behind and carried her suitcase downstairs.

'You should have waited for Jorge to do that,' Roberto said with displeasure.

'I've left the heavy stuff to him. Is everything arranged?'

He nodded. 'The men will keep a low profile by day and make regular rounds by night. Any intruder will meet with a nasty surprise.' Roberto picked up his stick. 'Now there are men to guard us, will you walk with me in the garden for a while, *carinha*? It will be good to exercise my leg before the journey.'

'I'd love to. I'll take my camera.' Katherine gave him a worried look as they went down the veranda steps. 'Will you manage some kind of exercise on the plane?'

'I will annoy the other passengers by much walking in the aisle.' He slanted a gleaming look at her. 'Perhaps a female flight attendant will hold my hand.'

She raised a cynical eyebrow. 'They'll be falling over themselves for the privilege.'

'You are so good for me!' He caught her in his arms and kissed her. '*Querida*, it is so hard to part with you.'

Katherine's throat was too thick with tears for speech. Get a grip, she told herself. Behave like a grown-up.

They both fell silent as they made their slow way back. Katherine paused to take some shots of the beautiful house, and asked Roberto to pose for her.

'And don't turn your good side to me,' she ordered. 'I want you just the way you are.'

She took several shots of him, and then let him take some of her, feeling as though her heart was being torn in half. Roberto was right. It took no time at all to fall in love. She'd managed it the first time she'd set eyes on him, something she'd previously believed happened only in fiction. But it was no reason to go haring off to Brazil with him. Roberto wanted her, she knew only too well. But whether his heart was in tune with his body was a different matter. Roberto Rocha was long accustomed to girls who took one look and fell in love with him. Or at least fell into bed with him.

When they finally set off Katherine craned her neck to take one last look at the house as the car moved down the winding drive. Her time at the Quinta das Montanhas had been short, but it had changed her life.

Roberto slid an arm around her and drew her close. 'Do not look so sad, *amada*. I will bring you back here one day, I promise.'

Not going to happen, thought Katherine miserably.

'When you reach Heathrow, please seek help with your luggage,' he ordered.

'I'll take a taxi and text Rachel. She'll be waiting as I get home.' Katherine smiled brightly. 'She's a journalist, by the way, so she'll want every last detail about my stay here.'

'Will you tell her about me?'

'Of course. But only about your home and past career, and the painting, not—'

'That I am your lover?' He put a finger under her chin to bring her face close to his. 'Because that is exactly what—and who—I am, *linda flor*,' he whispered against her parted lips, and kissed her with a heat she returned in kind. 'I will not make a spectacle of you at the airport,' he said unevenly, 'so this must be our goodbye. When I get home to the Estancia there are things I must do. When I have achieved them, I will come to you.'

The drive to Oporto ended all too soon for Katherine. When they arrived at the Francisco Sá Carneiro Airport Jorge stacked her luggage on a trolley and shook her hand very formally.

'*Boa viagem, Doutora.*'

She smiled warmly. 'Goodbye, Jorge. You and Lidia have been so kind.'

'*Sempre as seus ordems,*' he assured her, and with tact left them alone together.

Roberto took Katherine's hand, his eyes holding hers. 'I may come no further with you, *amada*, so go. Go *now*, before I drag you back to the car and take you to Brazil.'

She chuckled, as he intended her to, and laced her fingers with his. 'Goodbye, then.'

He raised her hand to his lips to kiss it, then with a sudden groan pulled her into his arms and kissed her mouth as though his life depended on it. '*Ate logo*, Katherine. I refuse to say goodbye.' Roberto put her away from him, breathing hard. 'Now go, *por favor*. And do not look back.'

Katherine obeyed blindly. The sheer physical pain of parting with Roberto left her feeling numb, not only during the longueurs of Security and Check in, but throughout the entire time she sat pretending to read a book while she waited to board the plane. It was only when she accepted tea later from a stewardess as the plane cruised towards Heathrow Katherine realised she'd sat through takeoff and the climb to altitude without even noticing. She shook her head in astonishment, surprising the man sitting next to her. Falling in love had strange side effects. But now she'd done so at long last, why couldn't she have fallen for someone who at least lived on the same continent?

Rachel came hurrying out of the house in Parsons Green when the taxi arrived and took charge of some of the luggage as Katherine paid the driver. Once everything was hauled inside the flat, Rachel gave Katherine a hug, eyeing her closely.

'I'll put the kettle on. Alastair's playing golf with Hugh, so we can chat in peace over tea and cakes.'

'Thanks, Rachel. The unpacking can wait.' Katherine yawned. 'I feel very lazy.'

'You look shattered. Surely you're not going straight back to work tomorrow?'

'I'll see how I feel in the morning.'

'But exactly how *do* you feel?' demanded Rachel. 'I'll make tea before you tell all. And I do mean all!'

Katherine curled up in a corner of the rubbed old leather sofa of her childhood while Rachel was busy in her kitchen and gratefully accepted the tea, but turned down the pastries. 'Could I postpone those until later?'

Rachel smiled in sympathy and sat opposite in the matching armchair. 'Bad flight?'

Katherine shook her head. 'Just tiring.'

'You look done in,' accused her friend. 'Was it hard work restoring the painting?'

'No.'

'Just no?' demanded her friend. 'Come on, Dr Lister. Give. What's wrong? If you don't tell me I'll explode.'

'I had such a lovely time it was a wrench to leave the

Quinta das Montanhas,' said Katherine with perfect truth.

'The house of the mysterious Mr de Sousa! What's he like?'

'Charming.'

Rachel's eyes narrowed. 'Come on, I want more than that. I take it he has money if he paid for your services, Doctor, but is he young, old, single or attached, thin, fat, bald—?'

'Divorced. Early thirties, slim, dark curling hair.'

Rachel was small and delicate-looking, but with a shrewd brain under her stylish blonde bob, and she'd known Katherine since they were teenagers. 'You liked him a lot.'

'Yes.'

Rachel's blue eyes narrowed in frustration. '*Talk* to me. Tell me what happened to make you look so down. I'm worried!'

Katherine obediently gave an account of her stay at Roberto de Sousa's glorious house, beginning with the first encounter.

'He was expecting a man?' Rachel chuckled. 'You must have been a nice surprise, then.'

Katherine shook her head. 'Not at all. Roberto didn't want a woman. Particularly a starchy art historian in glasses, with hair scraped back and so on.'

'You were on first name terms from the start?'

'Almost. He insisted on it.' Katherine went on to describe her excitement as she identified an early Gainsborough, followed by excitement of a different kind when she discovered that her host was better known as Roberto Rocha, one-time star of the racing circuit. 'But motorsport is not my thing, so I'd never heard of him.'

'*What?* You're kidding!' Rachel's eyes widened. 'I once had a fling with a sports journalist who wept when Roberto Rocha retired so young. Damn it, Katherine, I wish I'd been there with you to interview him—sorry, love, keep going.' She listened without interruption until Katherine finished, and then shook her head in wonder. 'It's happened, hasn't it? You've fallen hard for a man at last. Are you going to see him again?'

Katherine smiled bleakly. 'Not easy when we live on different continents. Besides, he'll probably forget all about me once he's back on the ranch.'

'As if!' said Rachel scornfully. 'I must look him up on the Net. I want to see this man for myself.'

'I've got some photographs on my laptop. Boot it up if you like.'

Rachel leapt to the desk to switch on the machine, and let out an inelegant whistle as the first shot came up. She turned the laptop screen towards Katherine.

'Is this the house?'

'Quinta das Montanhas, his holiday home in Portugal. The family home is on a ranch in Rio Grande do Sul, in Brazil. And that's Roberto,' said Katherine, her heart contracting as the next shot came up to show him smiling at her from the screen. 'I had to persuade him to let me take the photograph.'

Rachel eyed the image in silence for a moment, then turned to her. 'He's hot! And from the look in his eyes, Roberto's pretty hot for you, too.'

'We only met a few days ago.'

'What difference does that make?'

Katherine watched as Rachel slowly scrolled through the rest of the photographs, then, unable to bear looking at them any longer, asked her to switch the machine off.

'You do realise,' said Rachel, complying, 'that your

holiday snaps could be a nice little earner for me if I wrote a feature to go with them.'

'Yes. But you won't.'

'Sadly, no.' Rachel smacked her lips. 'Pretty lad, your Roberto.'

'He thinks his scar makes him ugly.'

'Wrong! It's hugely sexy. And those eyes smouldering as you snapped him! No wonder you fell for him. Who wouldn't?'

Katherine laughed for the first time, and Rachel nodded in approval.

'That's better. Alastair and Hugh are bringing food home, and I've laid the table for four upstairs.' She held up a hand. 'Don't say no. You'll sleep all the better afterwards.'

Katherine actually wanted nothing more than to crawl into bed. 'Just for an hour. But before I scrub myself I'd better do some unpacking.'

'Hurry up, then,' said Rachel promptly. 'See you upstairs about seven.' She turned at the door. 'Did you let the legal eagle know you were coming home today?'

Katherine stared at her in dismay. 'Oh, Lord, I forgot—I'll text him now.'

She was wielding a hairdryer when her doorbell rang later.

'Welcome home!' Andrew boomed through the intercom. 'Let me in.'

She released the lock and opened her sitting room door, standing back as Andrew strode in, brandishing a sheaf of flowers, sleek of hair, smartly dressed, and just slightly overweight. Or maybe that was just the contrast with Roberto. She stood still, bracing herself for an unpleasant few minutes.

'Hello, there,' he said, smiling, and waved a hand in front of her face. 'Earth to Katherine.'

'Hello, Andrew,' she said without warmth. 'I'm afraid you've caught me at a bad time. I'm getting ready to go out.'

He frowned. 'But surely you've just got home.'

'I have.'

He handed her the flowers. 'I brought these as a peace offering.'

'Thank you.' She put them down on a table.

He eyed her askance. 'What the hell's wrong with you, Katherine? You can't be jet-lagged after a flight from Oporto!'

'I'm just tired.'

'So how come you're going out?'

'I'm not. I'm having supper upstairs.'

'With the usual suspects, of course,' he sneered, but hastily changed tack in response to her glare. 'Katherine, if I was out of order before you went away, I'm sorry. But I feel I had every right to be annoyed when you took off the very day I had gala tickets for Glyndebourne.'

'I disagree,' she said coldly. 'Your behaviour was unpleasantly immature, Andrew.'

His light blue eyes opened wide in sudden fury. *Immature?* That's rich. If anyone's immature it's you, Katherine. It's time you left this student squat of yours and shared my house.'

'This is no squat, it's my family home. Besides, you just want me to share your bed,' she retorted, and could have kicked herself when heat leapt in his eyes.

'I'll share yours, if you prefer!'

She shook her head. 'Not going to happen, Andrew.'

His eyes turned ugly. 'Oh, yes, it is.' He seized her

by the shoulders, shaking her slightly when she winced in distaste. 'I've had it up to here with your teasing.'

'Teasing?' she hissed in outrage as his fingers bit into her flesh, then flushed in hot embarrassment as Alastair and Hugh burst into the room with Rachel close behind. Andrew dropped his hands, staring defiantly as both men, fit muscular six-footers, stood shoulder to shoulder to face him.

'Did he hurt you, Katherine?' asked Hugh in a deadly quiet voice.

'Say the word and I'll throw him out,' ordered Alastair, his Scots accent more pronounced than usual.

'Absolutely not,' she said irritably, and turned to Andrew. 'Time you were leaving, I think. It's not the way I would have chosen to say goodbye, but goodbye it is. It would never have worked out for us.'

He made a move towards her but stopped in his tracks at the look Alastair gave him. 'All right, all right, hold your horses. Look, Katherine, I'm sorry if I hurt you. I apologise, abjectly. Will you forgive me?'

'Yes.' She managed a bleak little smile. 'But it's still goodbye, Andrew.'

CHAPTER EIGHT

'MY GOD,' said James Massey when Katherine arrived at the gallery the next day. 'You look terrible. Not my flu, I hope!'

'No. There was a welcome home party last night, so I got to bed a bit late. Are you recovered, James?'

'Yes, thank God.' He smiled warmly. 'I owe you big time for stepping in for me, Katherine.'

'I was only too glad to help. Now, where's my young man?'

Katherine's heart gave a thump as she looked at the painting. Fully restored, the likeness to Roberto was unmistakable. 'When are you sending it off?'

'I'll wait to hear from the client.' James eyed her over his spectacles. 'So how did you get on with Roberto Rocha de Sousa?'

'Rather well,' she said sedately. 'He was very kind. So were the people who work for him.'

'You're not sorry I sent you to him, then,' he said slyly.

'No,' said Katherine with perfect truth. 'It was a very interesting experience.'

A day back in routine was oddly comforting after the emotional highs and lows of the past week. Katherine immersed herself in work so completely James had to remind her it was time to go home. Panicking at the thought of missing Roberto's call, she ran for the Underground, joined the crush of commuters on the train home and rushed into the house with just time enough to make some coffee while she waited for the all important phone call.

But the phone remained silent. As the evening wore on with no word from Roberto Katherine's emotions ranged from desperate disappointment to white-hot anger, which finally died into the cold ashes of bitter resignation. It was the oldest story in the book. After the accident, Roberto had been without female company and fate had sent her to him just when he needed a woman most. Probably any reasonably attractive woman would have done. But Katherine Lister had just happened to possess that certain something extra—insider knowledge of the subject that interested him most. Plus a response to his lovemaking that clenched her fists in fury at the thought of it. She'd even owned up to feelings for him! Though looking at it with the cold clarity of hindsight, she suspected that had been for her own sake as much as Roberto's. After all, she had a reputation to uphold. Other people might fall into bed with changing partners with joyous abandon, cerebral feelings or not, but never the famously choosy Katherine Lister. Who now knew that choosy had been nothing to do with it. With others, up to and including Andrew Hastings, she just hadn't been sufficiently attracted. Whereas one look at Roberto Rocha de Sousa had fired up the pilot light under her hormones, igniting a response she had never experienced before. And never would again.

It was a long, long week. Katherine's absorption in the work she loved passed the daytime hours at reasonable speed. But the evenings were bad. Rachel was the only one who knew just how bad. The weekend was bearable, courtesy of an invitation to Sunday lunch with Charlotte and Sam, where Katherine's trip to Portugal was the main topic of conversation over the roast. But however empty the evenings during the following week, Katherine felt no regrets about giving Andrew his marching orders.

'He said I was a tease,' she told Rachel.

'Because you said no?'

'Apparently.' Katherine scowled. 'I should have said no to Roberto, too.'

Rachel's eyes widened. 'You mean you actually... um...slept with him?'

'Yes. Literally. I was the only one on the upper floor of the house, and after the threatening letter came he refused to let me sleep alone and unprotected up there. So Roberto shared my room. And my bed.'

'To protect you. New approach!'

'At the time I was very grateful. I didn't fancy lying awake all night, afraid someone might climb through the window and mug me.' Katherine shrugged. 'It was no big deal.'

Rachel gave her a troubled look. 'Is that true?'

'No, damn it, it's not. For me it was a great big deal.' Katherine's eyes glittered coldly. 'But obviously not for him. And that, Rachel Frears, is the last time I mention his name, I promise.'

Two weeks to the day of Katherine's return, the phone rang while she was picking at a solitary supper.

'Katherine?'

She stiffened. 'Who is this?' Though she knew very well.

'Roberto. Roberto de Sousa,' he added when she made no response.

She rubbed a hand over the heart turning cartwheels at the first sound of his voice. 'Why, hello. You got home safely, then.'

'A week ago,' he informed her.

A *week* ago? 'You sound tired.'

'Just a little. Tell me, Katherine, how are you?'

'I'm very well,' she said untruthfully. 'How are you? Did your leg stand up to the flight?'

'No. *Infelizmente*, it gave me hell. When my father met me at the airport he insisted on taking me straight to the hospital, where work was done on it which much improved it, *gracas a Deus*.'

'That's good news. I'm glad for you.'

'I stayed at the hospital for treatment for a while. I did not ring you while I was in the hospital because I am well known there, you understand, and I was never alone. There was much to say to you that could not be overheard. So. *Escuta*—listen, Katherine.'

'I'm listening.'

'I had much time to think in the hospital, even more now I am back at Estancia Grande. You know that when Luis died it was my intention to stay at the Estancia only until I could leave to resume my career. But the crash changed that.'

'And now you're resigned to knuckling down to life on the Estancia?'

'*Exatamente*—as I always intended to one day. My father has bought my mother an *apartamento* in Porto Alegre, so that once I am fit enough to take over from him, they can spend time together in the city occasionally.'

'How do you feel about that?'

'I am glad for my parents, but I will be lonely here

without them. I miss you, Katherine,' he added with
sudden urgency. 'Have you missed me?'

'I wondered why you hadn't rung,' she admitted, her
mouth twisting at the understatement.

'You thought I no longer cared?'

'You never said you did care, Roberto.'

'*Como*?' he said, amazed. 'You did not hear the
things I said as we made love?'

'They weren't in English so I assumed they were just
the usual things men say.'

'They were not,' he said hotly, and paused for a
moment. 'You said you had feelings for me. Were they
just these usual things, also?'

'Whatever they were, they changed when I didn't
hear from you.'

'You thought that once we parted I forgot you?' he
demanded.

'Something like that, yes.'

'How could you think such a thing? I have never felt
such rapture in a woman's arms before, Katherine.'

'That's hard to believe when you subject me to a
fortnight's silence before informing me of the fact,' she
snapped, suddenly so angry she wanted to hit something.
Preferably Roberto de Sousa, bad leg or not.

'You are angry with me, *querida*,' he said with satisfaction. 'So you still care a little, yes?'

She took in a deep breath. 'Why didn't you get in
touch?'

'I was…not well for some time,' he admitted, so reluctantly Katherine smiled a little. Roberto the gaucho
obviously hated to confess to weakness. 'I wished to
feel better before I spoke to you. Also, I have had much
to think about before I talked to you.'

'So talk.'

'You sound like *Doutora*, not my Katherine.'

'Probably because I'm not your Katherine!'

'You have gone back to your lover?' he demanded.

For a moment she was tempted to say yes. 'No,' she said shortly.

'*Por que*? Why, Katherine?'

'You know why.'

'Because you love me!'

'Because I didn't want to leave my house to live in his.'

'You must leave it one day, when you marry,' he said, surprising her.

'Not necessarily. The lucky man could just live here with me.'

'You would insist on that?'

'Probably. But since I'm not about to marry anyone, the question doesn't arise. The painting's ready, by the way,' she added, to change the subject.

'That is good...*momento*.' He broke off to speak to someone in the background. 'Forgive me, I must go, Katherine. I will ring you tomorrow. Is this time of day good for you?'

'Yes, but not tomorrow,' pride forced her to say.

'Then I will ring the next day. *Ate logo*, Katherine.'

'Goodbye,' she said politely.

She spent the rest of the evening alternately elated because Roberto had rung at last, and furious because she'd postponed another call for an entire day, just to save face. To pass the time the following evening, she did some late night grocery shopping before going home, then ground her teeth in frustration when she got back to a message on her phone from Roberto.

'I wanted to speak to you before you went out, Katherine. I shall ring again tomorrow. *Dorme bem*.'

Rather to her surprise, Katherine did sleep well and got to work earlier than usual so she could leave on time with a clear conscience. She was determined to be at home early enough to sit calmly with a sandwich and a cup of coffee when the phone rang, which it did, prompt to the minute.

'Katherine?'

'Yes, Roberto.'

'*Otimo*, I do not like speaking to a machine.'

'I told you I wouldn't be at home last night, so why did you ring?'

'To hear your voice, Katherine. And I did, but only on the message on your telephone. You have had a busy day?'

'Yes. I think I've found something interesting for James to follow up, a possible sketch by Etty. Have you heard of him?'

'No. Tell me about him. What is he famous for?'

'Nudes,' she said reluctantly.

Roberto cleared his throat audibly. 'I will look him up. But no woman he has painted could be more beautiful than you, Katherine.'

'How kind of you to say so,' she said primly.

He laughed softly. 'That was Dr Lister speaking, *nao e*?'

'And, still speaking as Dr Lister, shall I tell James to ship the painting right away?'

'Yes, Katherine. Then it will arrive in good time for my parents' wedding anniversary at Christmas. I shall also give them the unknown young lady in white to make the pair.'

So his parents were the lucky recipients. 'I'll tell the shippers to take extra care,' she promised. 'How many years have your parents been married?'

'Thirty-five, Katherine—a triumph compared to my record! I shall arrange a *festa* to celebrate such an achievement, with all our friends and neighbours invited to a traditional *churrasco*.'

'Sounds like fun,' she said, feeling wistful.

'How do you celebrate Christmas, Katherine?'

'Very quietly.' It was the time she missed her father most of all. 'Beforehand, there's a lot going on socially, but I spend the day itself with my aunt and her husband.' And then return home in the evening to a house more than usually empty because Rachel, Alastair and Hugh would be with their families.

'My mother is most interested in the lady who identified my painting,' said Roberto. 'Therefore, it would please her very much if you came to stay with us at Christmas.'

Katherine's eyes widened. 'To Brazil?'

'It is where I live,' he said dryly. 'Come to me and see how we gauchos live here in Rio Grande do Sul. Say yes, Katherine.'

It was a tempting thought, but impossible, of course. 'It's good of you to invite me, but I can't take any more time off, Roberto.'

'If you could have this time, you would come?'

'I suppose I might,' she said cautiously.

'You do not wish to see me again?' he demanded. 'I was just a...how do you say...a fling?'

'I don't do flings,' she snapped.

'Then come,' he ordered. 'I will give you time to think about it, then ring you tomorrow.'

Katherine thought about it so much she had a restless night, unable to get round the fact that Roberto had taken two whole weeks to get in touch with her. Whatever treatment he'd had, or thinking he had to do, surely he could have just rung to say he'd arrived, if nothing else. But then, she reminded herself, she didn't know Roberto de Sousa well enough to understand the workings of his mind.

She learned a little more about those workings when she arrived at the gallery the next morning. James called her into his office to inform her that he'd received a request from Roberto de Sousa to allow Dr Lister two weeks holiday over Christmas to travel to Rio Grande do Sul. First class travel expenses would be provided.

Katherine eyed him narrowly. 'What did you tell him?'

He grinned. 'I said yes, of course. You'd be mad to turn down a free holiday in Brazil!'

Rachel said the same when Katherine rang her at lunch time. 'Just go, girl. You know you want to!'

Katherine did want to, but couldn't bring herself to let Roberto know that. Yet. 'You went over my head,' she accused when he rang.

'*Como*? I do not understand,' he said, surprised.

'You contacted James about giving me time off before I'd even agreed to come.'

'But you said you would consider it if you had the time off, Katherine, so I contacted Senhor Massey to... to expedite matters. This is right?'

'The word is right, yes.'

'My mother will write to you to invite you formally, if this is your problem, Katherine.'

'How kind of her.'

'So you will come?' He paused as though waiting for her answer. At last, in a harsh tone she'd never heard from him before, he said, '*Muito bem*, if you do not wish to see me again, forget it.'

'Hold your horses,' she said, panicking.

'*Como?*'

'I do want to see you again,' she said, climbing down. 'But if you want the truth, Roberto, I'm still hurting because you took so long to ring me.'

'I wanted to be strong again before I spoke to you,' he said harshly. 'Can you not understand that, Katherine?'

'Is that because you're a gaucho?'

'No, *querida*, because I am a man!'

'As I well know,' she assured him, and he laughed softly.

'So make me a happy man, and say you will come to me at my home, Katherine.'

Suddenly she wondered why she was dragging her feet. Of course she would go. Life was too short to pass up a chance like this. 'Since you put it that way, yes, I will, Roberto. Thank you very much for inviting me. I'll be happy to spend Christmas at your Estancia.'

There was silence for a moment. *'Gracas a Deus,'* said Roberto huskily. 'I shall be counting the days until you arrive. Tomorrow you must tell me which day you can leave and I will arrange a plane ticket.'

Once everything was settled after a prolonged and satis- factory talk with Roberto the following night, Katherine asked Rachel to an impromptu meal with Alastair and Hugh, and to their astonishment served champagne with rare fillet of beef.

'I know it should be red wine with this, but who cares?'

'This is obviously a special occasion,' said Rachel. 'What's up?'

'I'm going away for Christmas,' Katherine informed them.

'That's a few months away,' Alastair pointed out.

'True, oh, obvious one.'

'Are you going back to Portugal?' asked Hugh.

'No, to a cattle ranch in Rio Grande do Sul,' said Katherine with drama.

'To stay with Roberto Rocha!' Rachel announced, and then howled with laughter at the look on the men's faces. 'That's the mysterious client who paid Katherine to identify his painting.'

'Hold on!' said Hugh. 'Are we talking about the Brazilian racing driver here? The glamour boy who retired young?'

'The very same,' said Katherine, and smiled demurely. 'He's interested in my kind of work.'

'From what I remember, it's probably not only your work he's interested in, Dr Lister,' said Alastair, grinning, and then sobered. 'You'd better watch your step.'

'I'm staying with his parents, so it's all very respectable,' she assured him. 'And I'm travelling in style. Roberto's arranged a first class airline ticket.'

Once the urgent matter of the Christmas visit was settled with Roberto, during their regular phone conversations they caught up with everything that had happened in their lives since the parting at the airport in Oporto.

'The night we left the Quinta the security firm caught Elena's photographer friend searching my room,' Roberto told her. 'He swore on his mother's life that he was working alone, but I cannot believe that.'

'So once again the charming Elena gets off scot-free,' said Katherine.

'Let us speak no more of her. My interest is in you, Katherine Lister.'

Sooner than she would have thought possible, Roberto told Katherine he'd begun spending regular periods on horseback with the herd now his leg was so much improved. 'It will mean less frequent phone calls,' he warned. 'You sound tired, *querida.*'

'Life's a bit hectic right now, but I don't mind that. It makes the time pass more quickly until—' She stopped abruptly, not sure it was wise to show how much she longed to see him.

'Until we are together again? Tell me you share my impatience, Katherine!'

Of course she did. So much so she changed the subject in case he guessed how much. 'Roberto, have you any idea about your mother's dress size?'

'*Como*? How could I know that?'

'Think of me—'

'I do, constantly. Night and day!'

'Be serious.'

'I am very serious.'

'Concentrate. Is your mother something the same size as me? Is she dark, or fair, her eye colour and so on?'

'She is not quite as tall as you, and is just a little more...how shall I say...rounded? Her eyes and hair are dark like mine. Why?'

'I'm doing some Christmas shopping tomorrow.'

'You need buy nothing for me,' he said promptly. 'All I want for Christmas, Dr Katherine Lister, is to see you again!'

CHAPTER NINE

KATHERINE was seen off by Rachel and Alastair at Heathrow to catch her plane to São Paulo for the connection to Porto Alegre. The weather, which had been stormy for days beforehand, had relented to provide a still, frosty December evening for the flight.

'You'll get a bed in first class,' Alastair informed her. 'Or so my boss says. Never had the pleasure myself.'

There was a tearful hug from Rachel and a hearty one from Alastair before Katherine plunged into the long process of getting through Security on her way to her first experience of first class travel, the main advantage of which seemed to be fewer people and more space. When she finally boarded the plane she was surprised to find only fourteen passengers in first class. The flight would obviously be more comfortable than others she'd experienced, but for nights beforehand Katherine had been kept awake by increasingly cold feet about actually meeting Roberto de Sousa again. She had known him for such a short time that serious doubts had begun to creep in about the wisdom of flying halfway round the world to him. When they met again they might not feel the same intensity of emotion which had sent them into each other's arms so quickly at the Quinta das Montanhas.

But now she was here, fastened into her comfortable

seat, it was too late for doubts, and, once they had taken off and a meal was served, Katherine settled down to watch a film, with a Portuguese/Brazilian dictionary to study as backup.

She dozed, rather than slept, during the endless night and woke very early to visit one of the bathrooms to freshen up and change her clothes ready to disembark at seven at Guarulhos Airport in São Paulo. Leaving London in winter to travel to summer in Brazil had posed a problem about what to wear on arrival, and she had fallen back on jeans and matching jacket, plus a new scarlet T-shirt, to make sure Roberto spotted her straight away.

Over breakfast, Katherine learned she would have a good two hours to make the connection to Porto Alegre, and was glad of it later as she plunged into the noisy, colourful chaos of the airport to pass through Customs. The process was so bewildering and took so long she eventually reached the TAM check-in desk with very little time to board the plane.

When it touched down in Port Alegre later, Katherine took in a deep breath as she entered the great vaulted interior of Salgado Filho Airport. She'd made it! In spite of language problems, she managed to get to the baggage carousel, but because she was impatient it seemed to take forever before she was in possession of her luggage. Breathless with excitement, she decided to carry her bags and, having memorised the word for exit, made as fast a beeline for it as she could, laden with luggage. She came to a full stop when she reached it, her heart sinking when there was no sign of Roberto. Instead, with a feeling of déjà vu, she saw a stranger scanning the crowd as he held up a placard with her name on it. But this time there was no surprise when she presented herself. The man smiled, bade her welcome, showed her some identity and introduced himself as Geraldo Braga of Estancia Grande. He relieved her of her luggage and held out a letter. 'This will explain all, *Doutora*.'

Katherine read swiftly:

My son begs your forgiveness that he cannot come himself to greet you. He has been held up out with the herd. He asks that you trust yourself to Geraldo Braga, who will fly you here to Estancia Grande. My husband and I eagerly wait to welcome you. With kindest regards,
Teresa Rocha Lima de Sousa.

Katherine returned the letter to the envelope and smiled valiantly to hide her disappointment. '*Obrigado*, Senhor Geraldo.'

'If you will follow me, *Doutora*.'

Within a dizzyingly short time she found herself in a light aircraft with Geraldo Braga at the controls, and her excitement was intense as they soared up into the blue and left the city behind. When they eventually flew over vast grasslands her pilot gave her an approving smile as he saw her pleasure.

'Please to look down. We are now over Estancia Grande land, *Doutora*.'

She could see that the green of the rolling grassland had given way to something brown. 'What crop is that?'

'It is cattle. Estancia Grande cattle,' he added with pride.

'All that!' She stared down, amazed, at the great stain of brown on a landscape which eventually turned back into green grassland as they flew on.

'Soon you will see the house,' she was informed, and Katherine took in a deep breath, her excitement intense as he reduced speed to begin their descent. As they flew lower she saw a runway leading to a building that obviously housed the plane and, some distance beyond it on a rise, a large white house sheltered by trees, with other buildings nearby. The plane was set down so skilfully she could hardly believe they were on the ground when Geraldo got out of his seat to release her.

When he opened the door Katherine saw a man and a woman waving as they hurried towards the plane.

'*O Patrao* and Dona Teresa,' announced Geraldo, and leapt out with an agility she devoutly hoped she could copy. But the moment she was set on her feet Katherine was taken into a scented embrace as Teresa de Sousa bade her welcome with warmth that set some of her fears at rest.

'It is a great pleasure to meet you, Dr Lister,' she said in an attractive, husky voice. Elegant in tailored linen, Teresa de Sousa smiled warmly as she released her guest. 'This is my husband.'

He took Katherine's hand and, to her surprise, kissed it instead of shaking it. 'António Carlos de Sousa,' he announced. 'I add my welcome, Dr Lister.'

'Katherine, please,' she said, feeling absurdly shy.

'And I am Teresa,' Roberto's mother informed her and smiled at Geraldo. 'You will take the luggage, *por favor.*'

'*Agora mesmo*, Dona Teresa,' he assured her.

'I apologise for my son's absence,' said his father. 'He was much concerned when he was delayed.'

'He comes now,' said Teresa, the dark eyes so like her son's gleaming with anticipation as she turned to her guest. 'Watch, *cara.*'

Katherine looked in the direction of Teresa's pointing hand and realised that the noise she could hear in the distance was the thunder of hooves. As it grew nearer, her eyes widened in delight as a cloud of dust resolved itself into a group of riders who reined in their mounts in a sudden theatrical standstill. Antonio laughed softly behind her as one of the riders spurred his mount ahead of the rest, and sat easily in the saddle as he inclined his head in greeting. Like all the men behind him, he wore a flat hat with a chinstrap, a bandanna tied at the open collar of his loose linen shirt, balloon-pleated breeches and loose pleated leather boots with spurs. He swung down with lithe grace from the saddle, a revolver in a holster swung at one side of his silver-studded belt and a string of wooden beads and gleaming silver-sheathed knife at the other.

He swept the hat from his black curls and bowed, spurs chinking. '*Bem-vindo, Doutora*. Welcome.'

Katherine's heart thumped as she gazed at him. Was this gorgeous creature the man who'd limped his way round Quinta das Montanhas? 'Thank you,' she said quietly, and held out her hand.

Roberto bowed over it and raised it to his lips, gave her a look which turned her knees to jelly, and then turned to introduce her to his men. '*Doutora Lister de Inglaterra.*'

As one man they swept off their hats and smiled at Katherine, then one of them took the reins of Roberto's horse and, at his nod, the group wheeled round in a precise move and galloped away.

Teresa de Sousa smiled at her husband. 'Come, *querido*, we will hurry ahead and order tea while Roberto accompanies Katherine to the house. Do not linger too long, Roberto.'

The moment his parents were out of earshot, Roberto seized Katherine's hands. 'You came.'

She smiled slightly. 'As you see.'

'Until this minute, when I see you in the delectable flesh, I had doubts.'

'I said I would, Roberto.'

'After I used much persuasion!' His eyes glittered under the brim of his hat. 'Forgive me for my absence at the airport. I cursed the delay to high heaven. But I knew Geraldo would bring you safely to me.'

'And here I am,' she agreed, still afflicted with ridiculous shyness.

'*Gracas a Deus*,' said Roberto with feeling. 'I want very much to kiss you, Katherine, but I will not until we are alone.' He peered down into her eyes. 'Or do you not want to kiss me?'

'Not if it will give offence of any kind to your parents.'

'That does not answer my question,' he said huskily, and quickened his stride until she tugged on his hand to stop him.

'You're not limping!'

He smiled. 'At last you notice. I am better, no?'

'Better, yes.' She looked up into his face. 'And the scar is quite faint now.'

'But I am still not pretty enough to kiss?'

Katherine laughed and took his hand as he led her up the drive towards the big white building she could now see had two single-storey wings branching from the main house.

'You like our home?' asked Roberto, watching her face.

'It's beautiful.' Katherine was impressed. When Antonio de Sousa stole his bride away from her

Portuguese home he had brought her to a newer, but no less imposing house in Rio Grande do Sul. Roberto led her across a long colonnaded veranda into a large hall with a sweeping staircase and a tall, brightly decorated Christmas tree. He showed her into a comfortable room furnished with hide sofas and smaller, more feminine pieces upholstered in velvet and chintz faded enough in places to give the room a welcoming, lived-in look.

Teresa was waiting for them. 'You would like tea or coffee, Katherine?'

'I'd love some tea,' said Katherine gratefully, 'but first I'd like a very quick tidy up.'

'*Pois e.* Come. Antonio has gone to the *curral.* He will be back later.'

Katherine followed her hostess to a bathroom under the sweep of the curving staircase in the hall. After a quick session with the contents of her handbag, Katherine went back across the hall, smiling wryly as she passed the great tree. This was all a long way from her preconception of a cattle ranch. Teresa de Sousa smiled warmly as Roberto led Katherine to a seat beside him on a sofa.

'Are you very tired, Katherine?' he asked.

'A bit.' She smiled wryly. 'I feel as though I've been travelling for days.'

'I know this feeling!' Teresa shuddered in sympathy as she gave her guest a cup of tea. 'I changed planes twice on flight from Lisboa. Roberto did this also. When he arrived he was in great pain.' She smiled proudly at her son. 'He looks different man now.'

'But Katherine says she liked me before, even with my scar,' Roberto informed her.

'Because she is woman of intelligence.' Teresa smiled at her guest with gratitude. 'It was good fortune that

Senhor Massey sent you to the Quinta, Katherine. You liked my old home?'

'Very much. It's a glorious house. But so is this, in a different way, *Senhora*.'

'*E verdade*, but, please, I am Teresa.' Her eyes sparkled. 'I have so much to tell you about my recent discoveries. But not yet. First you must recover from your journey. And Roberto must go to his rooms for a bath. He smells of horse.'

He shot a gleaming look at Katherine. 'Did you enjoy the little demonstration I put on for you?'

'Immensely. It was superb horsemanship. Do the men here really dress like that all the time?'

Roberto nodded. 'To ride with the herd, yes, because it is the most practical dress. But otherwise the younger men wear jeans, ride motorcycles and drive pickups as in the rest of the country.'

'It was good of them to put on a show for me!'

He laughed. 'They were most happy to impress you.'

'And they did,' Katherine assured him. 'I'm honoured.'

Teresa got up. 'Come, Katherine. I take you to your room.' She shook her head at her son, who promptly rose to accompany them. 'You have your bath. I will take care of your guest, *meu filho*.'

With a wry smile, Roberto gave his graceful little bow. 'Be quick, then.'

Teresa de Sousa led Katherine up the curving staircase to a landing which ran the length of the upper floor. 'I hope you will like your room, Katherine.' She ushered her into a large bedroom at the far end. It was furnished in similar style to the Quinta, but in lighter wood which echoed the burnished coppery-gold of the polished floor.

To Katherine's surprise, the windows looked down on a flower-filled garden enclosed by tall hedges.

'How absolutely lovely,' she exclaimed, and smiled at Teresa. 'I didn't expect a garden like this at a cattle ranch!'

'It is all my work,' her hostess said, plainly delighted. 'When Antonio brought me here as a bride it was just grass and trees and the *curral* with the horses.'

'You've done it all yourself?' said Katherine, astonished.

Teresa laughed. 'I have help, but I am designer and *chefe*, and I work in it most days.'

'The flowering hedge is magnificent.'

'Hibiscus does well here. *Agora*, we must hurry, Katherine. There is your bathroom through that door, but now we return to my impatient son.' Teresa paused as they left the room. 'You like Roberto?' she said bluntly.

Katherine nodded. 'Very much.' Just to see him again had made it plain that 'like' didn't even begin to cover her feelings for Teresa de Sousa's charismatic son.

Teresa smiled mischievously. 'It is plain he likes you very much also, Katherine.'

Antonio de Sousa was chatting to his son over glasses of beer when they went down. As they got to their feet, Katherine saw that now Roberto was dressed in similar clothes to his father their physique was similar, but he had inherited his looks from his mother rather than from his equally handsome sire.

They had drinks on the veranda, but afterwards Antonio went off to his office to do some work, and suggested Roberto show his guest around the Estancia.

'Katherine might wish to rest on her bed,' Teresa protested.

Roberto got up quickly. 'Then I shall take her up to her room. Later, Katherine, we shall explore outside.' He took Katherine's hand to hurry her up the stairs. When they reached her room he closed the door behind him and took her in his arms, rubbing his cheek against her hair. 'Now we are here in private I can kiss you at last, if you wish, *amada*.'

'Of course I wish,' she said with a sigh, and surrendered to the mouth that devoured hers with such hunger she felt dizzy, her breath tearing through her chest as she inhaled the scent of Roberto's skin. As she felt him harden against her she pulled away, gasping. 'You'd better go now.'

'I know I must,' he groaned. 'Ah, *querida*, it is so good to have you here.' He trailed a hand down her flushed cheek as though convincing himself she was real. And then said the last thing she expected. 'Can you ride?'

She blinked. 'Ride?'

'A horse.'

'Oh. Yes. Though not recently.'

'*Otimo*. We shall ride together in the morning.'

'It's Christmas Eve tomorrow. Won't your mother mind if we take off?'

He shook his head. 'My mother is so delighted to have such a clever, charming guest she will not mind, I promise.'

When Roberto had torn himself away after demanding, and receiving, one last kiss, Katherine decided that the first thing on the agenda was unpacking. And found that the suitcases on the chest at the end of the bed were empty. She ran to the wardrobe, where every stitch of clothing she possessed was either hanging from the rail, perfectly ironed, or neatly folded on the shelves. She

raised her eyebrows as she stripped off her jeans and
shirt. The de Sousa family led a very different life from
hers! They were obviously conventional when it came
to relationships too, if Roberto had to kiss her in secret.
But since he had invited her here for Christmas, the de
Sousas must surely realise that there was more between
her and Roberto than just his gratitude for her work on
his painting. Katherine sighed as she leaned back against
the pillows on the pristine white bed, wishing he could
share it with her later.

Katherine shook her head in wry wonder. This was
something new in her life. Before meeting Roberto, her
attitude had been a take it or leave it view on the rare
occasions she'd found a man she liked enough to let
him make love to her. She'd had no idea how wonderful
the experience could be, given the right partner. Except
that Roberto, in almost every other way, was exactly the
wrong partner. He was now ready to put the glamour
and excitement of his past career behind him and settle
down to his share of running the Estancia Grande, but
there was no place in his kind of life for someone like
Katherine Lister.

She spent an hour deep in thought, then had a wash
and did her face, dug out a perfectly ironed pink shirt
and went down to the veranda.

'I sent for tea when I heard you,' said Teresa, and
smiled. 'You feel better now?'

'I do indeed. I was all set to unpack, but I found some
kind fairy had done it for me.'

Roberto held out a chair for her. 'Did you sleep?'

'No. I'm not one for naps in the day.'

'But you rested. Which was good,' approved Teresa.

'This is Dirce,' said Roberto, as the maid appeared with a tray. 'She unpacked for you.'

'*Muito obrigada*,' Katherine said to the girl, and Roberto explained briefly to the shy, smiling girl.

Knowing that Roberto was impatient to take her outside, Katherine drank down a cup of tea, excused herself to her hostess and went off with him to explore.

'I will not take you to my mother's garden,' said Roberto as they left the house. 'She will want to show you that herself. I will take you to the swimming pool, and then to the *curral* so you can meet some horses.'

'I'd better make friends with one if I'm to do some riding in the morning.'

'It is a long time since you rode?'

'Ages. So we'd better not go too far tomorrow or I won't be able to sit down to eat my Christmas dinner.' Katherine looked around her with interest as they made for a grove of trees which sheltered a sizeable swimming pool.

'You shall swim there later if you wish,' he told her and led her past it to make for the *curral*, a railed enclosure near a cluster of vine-covered outbuildings. She could hear men's voices and the sound of horses whickering, and she smiled up at Roberto in eager anticipation as they reached the group of horses tethered at the *curral* rails. Unlike the stable bred hacks she rode at home, these were the rough-coated descendants of wild mustangs, he informed her, stocky, strong animals with the stamina necessary for the hard work required of them. A group of men with dark, smiling faces came to greet Roberto, among them some Katherine had seen earlier. The head man patted one of the horses and beckoned politely.

'Geraldo is asking you to take a look at this one and see if you approve,' said Roberto.

Katherine climbed on the first rung of the rail so she could reach the horse's ears, and spoke into them softly while she stroked his head, telling him he was such a handsome fellow she'd like to ride him next day.

He whickered softly, and blew on her fingers, and Roberto laughed. 'I think he says he would like that very much. How could he not?' He called the other men over and introduced them. Katherine smiled warmly and greeted Geraldo again, then said *muito prazer* to Jose, Mario, Helio and Jango, and hoped she would remember which was which among the younger men.

'We will have a short ride tomorrow,' said Roberto as they strolled back to the house.

'Good. Other than not getting too stiff, I'd really like to help your mother.'

'Dirce and Maria the cook are already doing so, along with relatives they bring along for the occasion to help,' he assured her. 'Friends and neighbours will be sharing our meal, and preparation has been going on for days.'

She eyed him in alarm. 'I should have brought something grander to wear for the occasion.'

He laughed. 'Ah, Katherine. You may be a historian, but you are all woman also! And for this I am truly thankful,' he whispered in her ear.

'It's no laughing matter, Roberto Rocha de Sousa!'

He kissed her swiftly as they reached the trees near the house. 'It will not be the Christmas dinner you are used to, *amada*. It is a *churrasco* under the trees here, so no ball gown is necessary.'

'That's a relief.' Katherine eyed her feet in their flat

suede loafers as they approached the house. 'There's another problem, though, Roberto. No riding boots.'

'No matter. We will find some for you.'

Dinner that night was an informal affair on the veranda.

'We have simple meals on the days before Christmas, Katherine,' said Teresa. 'But on the day, our friends will join us for an Estancia Grande *churrasco.*'

'I wish you would let me help in some way,' said Katherine.

'After travelling so far, we cannot let you work,' said Antonio, filling her wine glass. 'And Roberto takes you riding in the morning. You ride at home?'

'Not as much as I'd like. When I was young I rode regularly at weekends and went on riding and trekking holidays with my father. These days, I just hire a mount when I have time.' She smiled at him. 'A different breed from your horses here.'

'Do not take her too far, Roberto,' warned his mother, eyeing Katherine with sympathy. 'It is recent that you lose your father?'

'No. Ten years ago, when I was eighteen.'

'He would be proud that his daughter is a *Doutora* of art history,' observed Antonio kindly.

Katherine nodded. 'He'd be delighted. Dad had a doctorate in the same subject, and lectured at the local college. He was at university with James Massey, the man I work for at the gallery.'

'And because of Senhor Massey I met you,' said Roberto with satisfaction.

After dinner Teresa led her guest across the hall into the formal drawing room for the first time, her excitement plain to see as she threw open the doors with a flourish. '*Olha*, Katherine. Here are the gifts Roberto has given us for our anniversary.'

'They arrived!' Katherine smiled in delighted recognition at the pair of paintings hanging either side of the massive stone fireplace. The young girl in her filmy white seemed to smile across shyly at the soberly dressed young man with the gleam in his eye. 'How marvellous! He looks really good now, Roberto!'

'Because you worked so hard on him,' he said, and kissed her hand. 'You are a clever lady.'

'*E verdade*, Katherine,' agreed his father, and smiled at his wife. 'Teresa wishes to tell you a story.'

Katherine was fascinated to hear that after Roberto mentioned his resemblance to the young man in the painting his mother had spent hours at her computer researching her family tree.

'Because of her research, some days we meet only at dinner,' said her husband dryly.

She gave him a sparkling glance. 'Better I am spending time with a computer than a lover, *nao e*?'

'Much better,' agreed her son fervently. '*Pae* would have killed him.'

'*E verdade,*' agreed Antonio, so matter-of-factly Katherine couldn't help laughing. 'Gauchos are jealous husbands,' he informed her with a gleam in his eye, then at an imperious look from his wife begged her to continue.

Teresa de Sousa's research had led her to José Luis Rocha Lima, an ancestor who had been involved in wine shipping in the late eighteenth century. 'He spent much time in England in a town called…how do you say it, Roberto?'

'Ipswich?' said Katherine in excitement. 'Where Gainsborough once lived?'

'*Isso mesmo.*' Teresa smiled triumphantly. '*Infelizmente,* I have no...no...'

'Provenance?'

'*Exatamente*, Katherine. I have no papers which prove the portrait is of a Rocha Lima.' Teresa took her son by the hand and led him over to stand underneath the portrait. 'But Roberto is proof enough, *nao e*? If I tie his hair back—'

Roberto dodged away, laughing. 'No ribbons, *por favor*!'

There was much animated discussion about the painting over coffee later, but at last Katherine had to smother a yawn, and Roberto jumped to his feet and held out his hand.

'You are tired, and if we are to ride in the morning we must go early. You still wish this?'

She nodded. 'If you can find me some boots, yes.'

'I have some which might fit,' said Teresa. 'But to rise early you must sleep now, *cara*.'

'What time must I get up?' asked Katherine, as Roberto took her up to her room.

'I will call you,' he promised, and took her in his arms as he backed into the bedroom door to close it. 'I want so much to make love to you, *amada*,' he whispered, and kissed her with a sudden, overwhelming hunger she responded to with equal heat.

'Me too,' she said breathlessly when she could speak. 'That's not going to happen, so go now, darling.'

Roberto's eyes blazed down into hers. 'I like this word. Say it again.'

'Darling—' Whatever else she'd intended to say was

smothered as his demanding mouth brought them to a mutual fever pitch of longing.

'This is torture,' he said hoarsely, and let her go. 'I will see you in the morning.'

CHAPTER TEN

KATHERINE was ready next morning when a tap on the door heralded not Roberto, as she'd expected—and hoped—but his mother, with two pairs of pleated soft boots, and Dirce following behind with a tray.

'*Bom dia*,' said Teresa, smiling. 'You are up early, Katherine.' She gestured to the girl to put the tray on the chest. '*Obrigada*, Dirce.'

'Good morning. I wasn't sure what time Roberto wanted to set off.'

'Soon, but only after you have eaten breakfast. Try the larger boots, *cara*.'

Katherine slid her foot into one and wriggled her toes. 'With socks, they'll be perfect.'

'*Muito bom*.' Teresa smiled. 'Roberto is impatient, but you must eat first.'

Katherine was as impatient as Roberto to set out on their ride together. After a sketchy breakfast she hurried downstairs in her borrowed boots and found Roberto on the veranda, spurs jingling in tune with his impatience as he talked to his parents. When Katherine joined them he swept off his flat black hat and bowed, looking so breathtakingly handsome in full gaucho dress again she laughed in delight.

'*Bom dia*, Katherine,' he said, preening outrageously. 'You like me in my working clothes?'

'I wish I had some just like them!' she assured him.

Antonio de Sousa handed her a black hat like Roberto's. 'You will need this, Katherine.'

'And do not take her far, Roberto,' warned Teresa. 'Katherine must be well for Christmas Day.' She turned to her husband, looking worried. 'Perhaps you should go with them, *caro*.'

He exchanged a look with his son, and shook his head. 'Roberto will take good care of our guest, *querida*.'

Katherine put the hat on and smiled at Roberto. 'Will I do?'

His eyes gleamed. 'Oh, yes. You will do.' After goodbyes and promises to be careful, Roberto seized her hand and hurried her off towards the *curral*. 'How are you today?' he asked, once they were out of earshot. 'Did you sleep well?'

'Not really. It was no effort to get up early.'

'Nor for me. I wanted you in my bed, Katherine.'

She stopped before they reached the *curral*. 'Is that your main reason for asking me here? The bed part, I mean?'

His eyes glittered under the black hat's brim. 'No. How could it be? I knew well that unless we were married, or at least *noivado*, my mother would not expect us to sleep together. I shall exercise much patience until we stay for a time in Porto Alegre before your flight home.'

Katherine eyed him narrowly. 'What will your parents think we're doing in Porto Alegre?'

'Shopping!' He led her to the horses, which were saddled and ready, waiting with two of the men in attendance. Katherine tried a careful greeting in Portuguese which won warm smiles, and went up to her horse to pat him.

'The saddle here is different from the English type,' Roberto warned.

Katherine found it had no cantle or pommel, just a simple sandwich of leather pads and woollen blankets with a thick sheepskin on top. But she would probably soon get used to it. The sun was already so hot she took off her sweater and put it in her saddlebag while Roberto buckled circular spurs to her soft boots. He handed her the reins and gave her a leg up, and she settled herself on the strange saddle, leaning to gentle the horse while Roberto adjusted her stirrups.

'In the past a gaucho rode barefoot,' he informed her, 'gripping the straps between the toes for balance.'

Katherine pulled a face. 'I'm *really* glad I don't have to do that. What's the horse's name?'

'Garoto, which means boy, *mais ou menos*—words you will hear often. They mean more or less.' He motioned her to follow as the other men rode off ahead of them.

'Do we need an escort, then?' asked Katherine.

'No. They go to work.' Roberto waved a gloved hand towards the horizon, where a sea of brown marked the presence of the herd. 'We go with them so you can meet some of the Estancia cattle.'

Soon Katherine was comfortable enough with the saddle and the gait of her horse to gaze in appreciation at the vastness of the landscape. 'What on earth does it feel like to know this is all yours, Roberto?'

'I feel proud! This is *minha terra*, my land,' he said, a possessive note in his voice as he swept a hand to encompass the rolling green of the pampas. 'At one

time, when Luis was still here, I had the freedom to
go off and prove myself in my racing career. But now I
am home to stay. My father is older than he looks, and
suffers a little with the blood pressure. So now he can
spend time at the apartment in Porto Alegre with my
mother, as she so much wishes, while I gradually take
over.'

'Is he happy about that?'

'It makes my mother happy, and he would do anything to ensure her happiness.'

Katherine nodded soberly, her eyes lighting up as they
grew near enough to hear the bellowing of the herd. She
watched, enthralled, battling to control Garoto's excitement as encircling horsemen and dogs drove the cattle
on, herding them through gates in the line of fences
she could now see demarcating the pastures. 'Amazing!
How many in this lot?'

'Several hundred head,' yelled Roberto, his teeth a
flash of white in his tanned face as he moved his horse
nearer. 'Stay by me!'

Katherine followed him as closely as she could as the
last stragglers were rounded up with much flapping of
the long white scarves used by some of the men. 'Will
they remain here now?'

'Because it is Christmas, yes, for the men to enjoy
the *ferias* with their families. Afterwards, they will be
driven to more distant pastures.' He cursed suddenly
as one of the riders broke away from the rest and came
riding hell for leather towards them.

'*Bom dia*,' called an unmistakably feminine voice
as the rider reined in her mount. Her eyes flicked over
Katherine's shirt and jeans, and dismissed them as no
contest for her own gaucho splendour.

'What are you doing here, Gloria?' demanded Roberto.

The huge dark eyes opened wide in innocence. 'I heard you had visitor. I came to meet her.'

'How do you do?' said Katherine. 'I'm Katherine Lister.'

'This is Gloria Soares, daughter of one of neighbours,' said Roberto briefly.

'I brought message from my father for Senhor Geraldo, who now wishes to speak to you, Roberto,' said Gloria. '*Va embora*. I shall share my coffee with Miss Lister.'

'She is Dr Lister,' corrected Roberto. 'Stay right here, Katherine. I will not be long.'

'I look after her,' promised the girl, and took a flask from her saddlebag as Roberto rode off. She unscrewed the cap and filled it with steaming liquid. 'Black. OK?'

Katherine nodded, and gentled her mount with a soothing hand as he sidled closer to the other horse. 'Thank you.'

'You stay here long?' asked Gloria, handing the cup over.

'Until after the holidays.'

'Then you get back to hospital?'

Katherine blinked. 'Oh...no. I'm not a medical doctor. I'm a historian.'

The girl stared at her blankly, then her face lit with a megawatt smile as she saw Roberto returning and she leaned from her saddle to grasp Garoto's bridle with an ungentle hand. 'Roberto is mine,' she hissed.

When Katherine fought to control the fidgeting horse the coffee spilled on the ground. She tossed the cup back to Gloria with a cool smile. 'Thank you. Goodbye.'

'Come, Katherine,' said Roberto, reining in between them. 'We must return. *Ate ja*, Gloria.'

'*Amanha*,' she retorted. 'Christmas Day.'

She saluted them with her whip, then reined her horse up on his back legs in a showy display, which was the last straw for Garoto. He went bolting off in fright, and Katherine bit back a scream and hung on for dear life on the unfamiliar saddle, with Roberto in frantic pursuit as they shot towards a stand of trees.

'*Katherine!*' yelled Roberto in warning.

She ducked instinctively to avoid low branches and the horse, completely spooked by this time, bucked her off and raced into the distance.

Roberto leapt from his horse and looped the reins over a branch, then fell to his knees by Katherine, demanding that she tell him where she was hurt.

'I'm…winded…not…hurt,' she gasped, when she could speak.

Very gently, he ran his hands over her arms and legs and, even more gently, along her ribs. Reassured there was nothing broken, he gathered her into his arms and held her carefully, his heart thundering against hers. '*Deus!*' he groaned at last. 'Gloria is too careless.'

But Katherine was only too aware that the girl had done it deliberately. 'Do I walk back?' she said, when she could breathe more easily.

Roberto shook his head. 'My horse will take both of us.' He kissed her swiftly. 'Can you get up now, *amada*?'

She nodded. 'Yes, if you help me.'

'Do not try to walk. Just raise your arms.' He picked her up and carried her to his horse. He spoke soothingly to his mount as he settled Katherine on the saddle, then swung up behind her. 'Lean on me, *carinha*.'

Katherine did so, gratefully. 'When we get back I'll have a hot bath and I'll be fine,' she assured him.

They had ridden only a short distance when Antonio de Sousa came thundering towards them.

'*Deus*, Roberto, *que foi*?' he demanded breathlessly as he reined beside them. 'When Garoto came back alone Teresa was sure Katherine had bad fall. Are you hurt, *cara*?' he asked, touching Katherine's hand.

'Only my dignity.' She smiled at him ruefully. 'I fell off.'

'You did not,' contradicted Roberto fiercely. 'The horse bolted, then threw you off. Did you examine him, *Pae?*'

Antonio was so upset that, with an apology to Katherine, he lapsed into Portuguese to explain. When he finished, Roberto looked furious as he translated.

'Garoto was bleeding from thorns on his neck when they unsaddled him. Did Gloria get near enough to do this?'

'*Gloria?*' exclaimed Antonio. 'That girl was out with the men again?'

Roberto nodded, and bent to Katherine. 'Did she touch Garoto?'

In no mood to be noble, she nodded briefly.

As they came in sight of the *curral* two young men came running to help. Antonio dismounted and held up his arms to take Katherine, but Roberto shook his head. 'I will carry her. She says she is not hurt, but before I let her walk my mother must examine her to make sure.'

Antonio nodded in agreement as, with great care, Roberto lifted Katherine down. 'My wife has much experience with broken bones.'

'I'm sure there's nothing broken. I can walk,' gasped Katherine, manfully ignoring her sore bottom.

'*Fica quieta*. I need to hold you,' said Roberto through his teeth, and kept on walking.

Teresa came running from the house, her English a little fractured as she demanded details, and Katherine let the stream of Portuguese from the de Sousas flow over her head, interrupting only to mention a bath as Roberto, breathing hard by this time, carried her up to her room, with Teresa following behind.

Roberto laid Katherine on the bed, for which she was deeply grateful. Sitting had no appeal for the moment.

'I will run a bath,' said Teresa, but Katherine shook her head, smiling ruefully.

'I'd rather a hot shower, please. I landed too hard on my behind to sit in a bath.'

'*Nossa Senhora!*' exclaimed Teresa in distress. She looked at her son. 'Go shower, *caro*. I will help Katherine.'

'I will come back soon,' Roberto assured Katherine, and kissed her with a ferocity that made his mother blink. 'When you fell off my heart stopped,' he said hoarsely.

She smiled reassuringly. 'At least I didn't fall on my head—but I'm afraid I lost the hat.'

Roberto said something so rude about the hat his mother protested and shut the door on him as she sent him away. With long experience of her menfolk's bruises, sprains and occasional broken bones, Teresa helped Katherine undress, then ran practised hands over her until she was satisfied nothing was broken.

'I just bruised my bottom,' Katherine assured her.

Teresa nodded, smiling in sympathy. 'We give you cushion to sit at table for lunch.' Her eyes darkened. 'It is time Ildefonso Soares kept Gloria on tighter rein.'

* * *

Once the meal was over time rushed by in preparation for Christmas Day. Teresa gave her afternoon nap a miss and excused herself to go off to the kitchen, and suggested Katherine recline on the veranda to watch Antonio and Roberto supervise the men who were setting up tables and chairs, and stringing lights among the trees. But after watching for a while Katherine went for a walk to avoid stiffening up. She left the veranda to make for the kitchen block and found a hive of industry inside. Teresa smiled in welcome.

'You need something, Katherine?'

'I want to help. Can I join you?'

'*Pois e!*' Teresa ushered her into the large, busy room, which was filled with savoury smells. '*Escuta*,' she said loudly, and the smiling faces turned as she spoke to them quickly in Portuguese. 'I told them you wish to help. You know Dirce.' The girl nodded, smiling. 'Here is her mother, Maria the cook and Lourdes, sister of Maria, and Ana and Zelia her daughters.' All the women smiled and murmured a shy *muito prazer*, then Maria and Lourdes went back to slicing up meat for the *churrasco*, while the younger girls fashioned small savoury pastries.

Teresa eyed Katherine hopefully. 'You can cook, *cara*?'

'Yes, though not on this scale. But there must be something I can do.'

'Another *sobremesa* for tomorrow would be good. Something English, perhaps?'

Katherine nodded, eyeing the fruits Dirce had sliced ready for a *salada de frutas*. 'I could make a couple of trifles.' She listed the ingredients she needed, and was soon whipping up a sponge cake for the base. While it was baking, she went on to the tricky job of making custard, and the time passed so quickly Katherine was in the cold room off the kitchen later, putting her trifles together, when she heard Roberto burst into the kitchen with a flood of questions for his mother.

'*Calma, calma*, she is in there!' said Teresa.

He strode into the room to glare at Katherine. 'I searched the house and could not find you!'

She smiled. 'I was just enjoying myself with the others in the kitchen. I live alone at home, remember.'

Roberto stood utterly still as he looked down into her eyes. 'You need never be alone again.'

They gazed at each in silence until at last Katherine managed a smile. 'I need to finish this.'

He kissed her swiftly. 'Do not be long.'

When they sat down later to a Christmas Eve dinner served early so that the maids could get off in good time, Katherine was deeply touched to find that Teresa had done her utmost to make her guest feel at home.

'Tomorrow we have *churrasco*,' she told her guest as Maria came in with a huge turkey on a platter. 'But tonight we eat British Christmas dinner.'

'You need more cushions, Katherine?' asked Antonio, eyes twinkling as he carved.

'Not right now, *obrigada*,' she said, laughing.

Once the food was distributed the maids were thanked and sent off. 'Tonight we clear away ourselves, because they return early in the morning with their families for the *churrasco*,' said Teresa, and raised her glass in toast. 'We wish you a most happy Christmas, Katherine.'

Katherine raised her glass to them, smiling in gratitude. 'Thank you so much for inviting me here.'

After dinner Teresa refused offers of help from her guest and told Roberto to take Katherine for a walk under the stars. 'This is one night of year Antonio helps me in kitchen,' she said, laughing at her husband.

Katherine hurried upstairs to exchange her heels for flat sandals, and rejoined Roberto on the veranda.

'I switched on the lights in the trees,' he told her, taking her hand.

'It's magical,' she said, then turned to him urgently. 'Roberto, I've brought Christmas gifts for your parents. Should I hand them over tonight?'

'In the morning is better, after breakfast. We eat this together at Christmas. Most other days we leave the house early, either to ride with the herd, or work with the men at the dehorning and castrating.' He laughed as she winced. 'It is a necessary part of life here.' He brought her round to face him as they left the lights behind, his face suddenly very grave. 'Does our life here seem alien to you, Katherine?'

'Different, not alien.' She smiled up at him. 'I've only seen cattle like yours in Western films before.'

Roberto pulled her close to kiss her and, as she responded with unreserved fervour, went on kissing her until they were both trembling. She tore her lips away at last and held his face in her hands.

'Tell me the truth.'

'*Sempre*—always,' he said with passion.

'Are you going to marry Gloria Soares?'

'*Como!*' Roberto held Katherine away by the shoulders, staring down at her in outrage. 'Are you *louca*? You think I would bring you here to meet my family if I was promised to another woman—which is wrong description for a spoilt child like Gloria!' His fingers suddenly bit into her skin through her dress. 'She said this to you today?'

'More or less. Just before she hurt poor Garoto and

did her rodeo act to make him bolt with me,' Katherine said hotly.

His face hardened with sudden menace. 'Tomorrow I will have words with Maria Gloria Soares.'

'You'd better keep her right away from me, Roberto de Sousa,' said Katherine tartly. 'I might be tempted to punch her nose in revenge for my bruise.'

He gave a delighted crack of laughter and pulled her close again. 'If we were alone,' he said in a tone which buckled her knees, 'I would be most happy to kiss your bruise better.'

She swallowed, and buried her face against his chest. 'That's not fair.'

'You have the saying that all is fair in love and war, *nao e*? And this is not war between us.' He tipped her face up to his, the look in his eyes impossible to mistake in the faint light coming from the trees.

'No,' she agreed, and stood on tiptoe to kiss him.

He returned the kiss with fervour, then raised his head as bells pealed in the distance. *'Escuta.* It is Christmas Day. *Feliz natal*, Katherine.'

CHAPTER ELEVEN

THE moment Katherine got up next morning she sent texts to Charlotte, Rachel, Alastair and Hugh, and was ready in good time when Roberto, in best gaucho gear, came to fetch her for breakfast. When she gave him a kiss and wished him a happy Christmas, he took her in his arms and kissed her fleetingly.

'It will be happy because you are here with me,' he whispered, and took her down to join his parents, who were in *festa* dress like their son for the breakfast which was served early so gifts could be exchanged before the maids arrived.

Katherine had given much thought to hers, and felt deeply relieved when Teresa expressed delight as she unwrapped a cashmere sweater and cardigan.

'*Que coisa linda*, cara. Thank you.'

Katherine smiled. 'When I learned that it snows here in winter, I thought this might be useful.'

'Useful? It is beautiful. I shall be so *chique*! You also, Roberto,' Teresa added as he held up the heavy Cambridge blue sweater Katherine had given him.

'I wish it was cold enough to wear it today,' he said and leaned to give Katherine a kiss. '*Muit'obrigado*, Katherine.'

She smiled apologetically as his father took a bottle

of venerable single malt whisky from its box. 'I'm afraid yours is not very inspired, Antonio.'

'It is great treat for me, *cara*,' he assured her, and smiled mischievously. 'But I shall hide it. I refuse to share with our guests.'

'You have not opened your present from Antonio and me, *cara*,' said Teresa. 'Were you so worried that we would not like your gifts?'

'Yes,' admitted Katherine honestly, then blinked, totally overwhelmed when she found her present was a gaucho outfit like the men's, complete in almost every detail—shirt, kerchief, *bombachas*, poncho, even spurs and a silver knife. The only thing lacking was the gun. 'How absolutely wonderful! Thank you both so much.'

'We could not buy the boots, but I think we have right size in everything else,' said Teresa with satisfaction.

'My gift is very small,' said Roberto and slid a tiny package towards Katherine.

She removed gold paper from a small velvet box which contained earrings of oblong emeralds suspended from diamond studs. She swallowed hard. 'Oh, Roberto!'

'You do not like them?' he demanded.

She flashed him a reproachful look. 'Of course I like them, but I didn't expect such...such...'

'Excellent taste?'

'Extravagance!' She got up to kiss him, and went round the table to thank his parents in the same way.

'They are perfect with your eyes, Katherine,' said Teresa, and looked at her son. 'Is why you chose them, *nao e*?'

He nodded. 'But I feared she might not accept them.

She was very angry in Viana do Castelo because I paid for some shoes!'

Katherine felt the blood rush to her face. 'That was different.'

'*E verdade!*' Roberto smiled triumphantly. 'You cannot refuse anything I give you today because it is Christmas. And today is *festa* day so you must wear them now. I will put them in for you.'

Katherine took the plain gold studs from her earlobes and let Roberto replace them with the emeralds, which looked so incongruous with her T-shirt she laughed up at him. 'Cinderella needs to change into her party dress. When do the guests arrive?'

'Any time from noon onwards,' said Antonio, smiling genially. 'Come, Roberto. We must check the fires in the *churrasco* pits.'

'Who does the actual cooking?' asked Katherine.

'Antonio and Roberto begin while Geraldo, husband of Maria, keeps fires burning,' said Teresa, 'then the other men take over.'

'Hurry to change your clothes, *querida*,' ordered Roberto. 'Wear the green dress!'

Katherine looked with admiration at Teresa, who had exchanged her normal tailored look for a full-skirted dress in white-dotted blue cotton. 'I shall look very ordinary in my plain little shift.'

'You will be *muito elegante*,' said Teresa firmly. 'But hurry, *cara*, the girls are here, ready to start frying the *empadinhas* they made yesterday.'

For Katherine the experience was so different from her normal quiet Christmas Day with Charlotte and Sam she had to pinch herself from time to time to make sure she wasn't dreaming. In flat gold sandals instead of heels, and with one of Maria's large white aprons tied over her green dress, she hurried back and forth with the smiling maids to lay the tables and take trays of sliced meat to put in cool boxes alongside Roberto, who looked so blazingly happy as he tended the barbecue pits Katherine found it hard to recognise the embittered, injured man she'd first met. A few minutes before noon Teresa took Katherine away to tidy up before the guests began to arrive.

'You do this every Christmas?' asked Katherine with awe, as they went in the house.

'For many years, yes.' The fine dark eyes shadowed slightly. 'But not last year after Luis died.' Teresa squared her shoulders. '*Agora* we celebrate that Roberto is recovered and happy. Life must go on, *nao e*?'

Normally not the most demonstrative of people, Katherine couldn't help giving her a little hug. 'Absolutely. From experience, I know it does.'

Beforehand Katherine had wondered at the quantity of food being prepared, but as guests arrived with children and, in some cases, grandchildren, along with the families of the men who worked on Estancia Grande, it was obvious why Teresa and her team had prepared for so many. Roberto and Antonio left their posts to greet their colourfully dressed guests, leaving Geraldo and his men to oversee the sizzling meat sending up a wonderful aroma into the air.

Roberto kept her close as his parents presented her to one group after another, his arm tightening round her waist when Ildefonso Soares, the last to arrive, came up with Gloria, striking in a flame-coloured number with more flounces on it than any dress there.

'*Calma, amada*,' murmured Roberto, as he felt Katherine tense. 'No fighting on Christmas Day.'

Katherine flashed him a sparkling look and gave both

the latecomers a radiant smile. *'Muito prazer, e Feliz Natal.'*

Gloria lunged forward, obviously intending to kiss Roberto, but he gave her cheek a pat and shook her father's hand.

'I come to help, Dona Teresa,' the girl announced, but Antonio shook his head, smiling.

'It is not necessary, *cara*. We have Katherine's help today.'

Ignoring Gloria's scowl, Teresa showed her to the place reserved for the Soares family at one of the tables, which were now loaded with festive food and drink.

Antonio de Sousa and his wife sat at the head of a table with the families of their men, with Roberto and Katherine at the foot. At first the women were shy, but as Roberto supplied rapid translations for Katherine's questions they grew more relaxed, and there was much laughter when he handed her his *cuia*, a gourd filled with *mate*, the local herb tea she was instructed to drink through his *bomba*, a silver spoon with a perforated bowl.

'It is a straw to draw up the mate,' he told her.

With expectant eyes on her she obediently sucked some of the hot liquid into her mouth, but as the taste hit her tongue her eyes opened wide, then watered with the effort to swallow the bitter brew instead of spitting it out. She shuddered and very carefully said, *'Nao, obrigada. Agua por favor!'*

Everyone laughed as Roberto passed her a glass of water. 'Well done,' he whispered, taking her hand. Katherine smiled up at him, intercepting a look from Gloria which should have killed her on the spot. 'We're attracting attention,' she whispered, but his grasp only tightened.

'I do not care.'

To Katherine's surprise, she didn't either and smiled as she got up in response to his mother's signal, as Teresa beckoned to Maria and her team to follow them as some of the men struck up music with guitars and accordions.

'We fetch the *sobremesas* now,' Teresa announced as they hurried into the house.

Maria, Dirce and the other women took bowls of fruit salad to the tables, along with ice cream for the children. Teresa took a great crystal bowl of cream-topped trifle to the table where the Soares family was sitting, and Katherine put the other in front of Antonio.

'Would you like to try some?'

Antonio gazed at the inviting confection with anticipation. 'With much pleasure, *cara*.'

Katherine's trifle was greeted with equal enthusiasm by all the adults on the table, including Roberto. Katherine smiled to herself as she saw Gloria deliberately push hers away untasted, much to the satisfaction of her father, who ate both portions with gusto.

By this time children were playing under the trees, with parents interfering only when things grew heated. Then suddenly the music changed, and every child was instantly alert as they heard the familiar strains of *Jingle Bells*.

'*Papae Noel!*' shrieked a small girl, and at once there was a mini stampede as the children flocked towards the white-bearded figure in red seated on a horse pulling a trailer filled with bulging sacks of presents.

As he dismounted with a loud, 'Ho-ho-ho!' the children swarmed around him in vociferous demand.

'*Calma, calma.*' He held up quelling hands and spoke

magic words which sent them scampering back to sit on the grass, gazing up at *Papae Noel* in expectation.

'Heavens, he must be hot,' murmured Katherine, utterly delighted by the scene.

'Not too much. His suit is thin silky fabric,' Roberto told her. '*Com licenca*, I must help my father give out the presents.'

As Father Christmas read out the names on the gifts, either Antonio or Roberto distributed them to the eager recipients under the indulgent eyes of parents and grandparents. When every child had a present, another sack was produced with small gifts which *Papae Noel* handed out to the rest of the guests, including one for Katherine. Roberto resumed his place beside her as everyone at the table opened their gifts, displaying them with cries of pleasure. Then all eyes turned on Katherine as she took the wrapping paper from a velvet box. She needed no translation to know that everyone was begging her to open it, and took out a gold chain with a pendant emerald which matched her earrings. She gave Roberto a startled glance.

'It is Christmas Day,' he reminded her, 'so you must accept it, Katherine.'

'Then I will. Thank you. *Muito obrigado*,' she repeated for everyone's benefit, then bent her head so Roberto could fasten the clasp.

At his signal, the music began again and many of the guests flocked to the space under the trees to dance, including Gloria Soares, scarlet frills fluttering as she commandeered centre stage.

Katherine was only too pleased to concede it to her, though after a while Roberto insisted she partner him in the dance she soon found easy enough, happy to follow his lead to an accompaniment of encouraging smiles from the other dancers. But from then on she sat with Roberto's parents while their son did his duty by some of the ladies, and finally danced with a triumphant Gloria. But her pretty, sultry face was stormy by the time she ran back to her father, and soon afterwards they were first to leave. Roberto stood with Katherine and his parents to say goodbye to departing guests as children were rounded up and sleeping babies carried home to bed.

Much later, after Maria and her team, helped by the Estancia hands, had cleared away all signs of the celebration, Katherine and Roberto said goodnight to his parents and before going to bed went outside for a walk under the lights twinkling in the trees.

Roberto took her hand. 'So, Doutora Lister, how did you enjoy your gaucho Christmas?'

'Immensely. It was such a lovely day.' She raised an admonishing eyebrow. 'Though you shouldn't have been so extravagant. My gift from Father Christmas caused quite a stir.'

He shrugged. 'It was just jewellery, Katherine—not a ring.'

The word seemed to hang in the air in the still, starlit night. She wondered how she would have reacted if it had been a ring, and all the implications that went with it, and experienced a pang of emotion hard to identify.

'So what happens here tomorrow, Roberto?'

'My parents will rest, the servants will have a holiday, and you and I shall spend more time together,' he announced with satisfaction. 'We shall go for a short ride—if a certain delectable part of you is better now.'

'It must be, because I haven't given it a thought all day,' she said, laughing.

He caught her close and rubbed his cheek against her hair. 'To have you here with me today is the best

Christmas present of my life.' He looked into her eyes. 'Until I actually saw you standing by the plane, I had doubts that you would come.'

'I had some myself,' she said wryly. 'It was a big step for me to fly all this way to stay with a man I'd known such a short time, Roberto. It didn't help when you weren't there to meet me, either.'

'I apologise for that, Katherine. I was furious when I got held up with the herd—though it gave me chance to put on my little show for you.' He smiled down at her. 'I wanted to impress my woman.'

Katherine eyed him narrowly. 'Is that how you think of me?'

'Yes,' he said simply. 'I believe fate meant us for each other.'

'Then it's a pity fate hadn't located us closer together,' she said ruefully. 'Sheer geography is a bit of a problem for you and me, Roberto Rocha de Sousa.'

'But we will find a solution.' He took her hand to walk back to the house. 'You must be tired. You have worked hard today.'

'I enjoyed it enormously. By the way,' she added, giving him a sidelong smile, 'what did you say to Gloria? She was not a happy girl after you danced with her.'

'I gave her hell for causing your horse to bolt with you.' Roberto shrugged. 'I also threatened to tell her father, which made her panic. Much as he dotes on her, Ildefonso Soares could not have forgiven her for causing harm to my guest—nor to my horse,' he added, smiling, and took her in his arms. 'Now, let us forget everyone else and enjoy these few moments together before we must go to our separate beds.'

CHAPTER TWELVE

FOR the rest of her stay at Estancia Grande, Roberto
ensured that Katherine experienced as much as possible of the gaucho way of life. She went riding with
him most days, an activity she enjoyed all the more in
her comfortable gaucho outfit. There were invitations
to barbecues with friends of the de Sousas, a traditional
gaucho dance for the festive season and even, to her
great delight, a day at a rodeo.

'They go on for many days, and Luis and I competed
when we were young,' Roberto informed her as he drove
her home. 'But only one day was possible for you this
time, since you leave the Estancia tomorrow. But we
have our stay in Porto Alegre before you fly away from
me, *amada*.'

'Your mother talks about the city a lot,' Katherine
told him, refusing to think about flying away just yet.
'In strictest confidence she told me she likes it almost
as much as Lisbon.'

He laughed. 'The highest accolade of all from Teresa
Rocha Lima!'

Dinner that night was an extra special occasion, with
every local delicacy Teresa could think of since it was
Katherine's last night at the Estancia.

'What will you buy when you do your shopping, *cara*?' she asked over the meal.

Shopping? Katherine went blank for a second.

'You mentioned presents,' Roberto reminded her.

She nodded hastily. 'For my aunt, and James Massey and his wife. And a few friends.'

'You will find much choice in Porto Alegre,' said Teresa, and sighed. 'It is sad that you must leave so soon. You must persuade Katherine to return soon, *meu filho*.'

Roberto smiled at his mother. 'I will do my very best.'

'And now,' said Antonio, rising, 'we will drink a toast to our guest. *Boa viagem*, Katherine.'

'Thank you.' She blinked hard and raised her own glass. 'To the de Sousa family for making me so welcome. It has been an unforgettable Christmas.'

There were more farewells next day when Katherine was ready to leave. She went into the kitchen to say goodbye to Maria and Dirce, and then took a walk to the *curral* with Roberto to say goodbye to the men there, and then to Garoto, who pushed his nose against her hand. Then Geraldo and Janio carried her luggage to the plane, where Antonio stood with an arm round his wife as Katherine kissed them goodbye. As Roberto took the plane up and away from Estancia Grande, she looked down through a blur of tears at the two figures growing smaller as they waved in farewell.

'You are sorry to leave, Katherine?' said Roberto.

'Yes,' she said tersely, her throat too thick to say more.

At the airport they took one of the orange town taxis, and Roberto asked the driver to take them on a short tour of the city on the way to the São Rafael Hotel. He helped Katherine into the back seat, slid in after her and pulled her close to kiss her hard the moment the taxi moved off.

'I needed that,' he said gruffly, and rubbed his cheek against her hair. 'I love my parents, you understand, but it is good to have you to myself at last, Katherine.'

'They were very kind to me,' she reminded him.

'My mother was a little nervous before you arrived, *carinha*.'

'Why?'

'Because you are a *Doutora Historiadora*, and there-fore very clever. She was expecting someone far more intimidating than you, Katherine. Although,' he added thoughtfully, 'if you had arrived wearing those severe clothes and the famous spectacles you would have fright-ened her to death.'

Katherine hooted. 'I haven't known your mother long, Roberto, but I can't imagine her feeling intimidated by anyone.'

'*E verdade!*' Roberto laughed. 'She was just a teenag-er when my father, who was fifteen years older, brought her here, but now she is very much *Dona da casa*, and rules Estancia Grande with a firm hand.'

'Your father adores her, and she him. It's heart-warm-ing to see them together.'

'Heart-warming,' he repeated softly. 'I like that.'

Katherine smiled at him, then turned to look out at the square they were entering. 'Come on then, Roberto de Sousa, do your tour guide bit.'

'*Sempre as seus ordems,*' he said promptly, and began rattling off information. 'We are in the Praça da Matriz, and that building with the large dome is the Catedral Metropolitana. Close by is the Palácio Piratini, the

Governor's residence, and to the north the Teatro São Pedro. There are many such buildings in the city but we shall leave them for another day.'

Not that there would be many more days. Katherine pushed the thought away as she craned her neck to take it all in.

'Now,' said Roberto firmly, 'we go to the hotel. You would like a little rest before lunch, no?'

'Actually, I'd like a shower. I got a bit hot in the plane. The flight was a lot more exciting with you in charge, Roberto.'

He grinned. 'You did not trust me to land you safely?'

She grinned back. 'I suddenly remembered that Roberto Rocha was at the controls!'

'I will have my revenge for such slander,' he threatened as they arrived at the hotel. 'I stay here when I am in Porto, my parents also. It is not as big as some of the modern hotels, but it has much character, also excellent food, and on the top floors there are suites with a view of the lagoon.'

The process of checking in went very smoothly with Roberto in charge. Katherine barely had time to look round a reception lobby with gleaming golden floors and big leather furniture before they were in a lift on the way to their suite, where Roberto led her into a charming sitting room.

'The luggage will arrive soon, but I need another kiss,' he informed her, closing the door behind them. He took her in his arms and kissed her, then raised his head to smile down into her eyes. 'I have dreamed of being alone together like this.'

So had Katherine, but for the moment it seemed unwise to say so. Though for some reason the brief kiss had dispelled the unexpected frisson of nerves she experienced at the glimpse of a large bed through the half open bedroom door. 'So show me this view, then.'

They went to the windows to look down on the great lagoon. 'The Lagoa dos Patos,' he informed her.

'Patos?'

'Ducks.'

She grinned. 'I expected something more romantic, like flamingos.'

Roberto shrugged in mock apology. *'Desculpe, senhora*, no flamingos.' He turned at a knock on the door. 'That is our luggage.' He went to tip the porter, then rejoined Katherine at the window and put his arm round her waist. 'Have you recovered from my flying skills enough to eat, *querida*?'

She nodded with enthusiasm. 'As long as I shower first before we go down.'

He tipped her face up to his. 'I suggest we ring room service for our lunch, and then tonight, when you have rested, we shall dine out. You would like that?'

'Of course I would, though maybe not *churrasco* tonight. I've eaten more meat since I came here to Brazil than I've had for months at home.'

'And here we have the best beef in Brazil, also the best way of cooking it.' His eyes gleamed. 'It gives a man strength—his woman also. Which bag do you need first?'

'The smallest.'

'I shall put it with mine at the foot of the bed.' His eyes met hers. 'You approve?'

Knowing he meant more than luggage, she nodded her assent. 'Now, where's this bathroom?'

After her shower Katherine wrapped herself in one

of the hotel robes and opened the door to see Roberto gazing down at the view. 'How long will lunch be?'

He spun round, his eyes eating her. 'I said half an hour. Shall we rest for a while first?'

'You're tired?'

'No, *amada*, I am not.' He gave her a look which melted her bones as he crossed the room in two strides to pick her up, and then stood laughing down at her with such blatantly male satisfaction she laughed with him. 'I can now do this, Katherine.'

'Indeed you can.' She rubbed her cheek against his as he carried her to the bed.

Roberto lowered her gently, then followed her down to kiss her with such sudden, explosive heat robe and clothes were soon tossed away as they came together at last on the wide white bed, her hunger a match for his as he made love to her with words she only half understood but with caresses which needed no translation as they set her body on fire.

'Since the moment I saw you again I have longed for this,' he said against her mouth.

'Then love me. Now,' she ordered huskily, and Roberto gave a stifled elated laugh and united them with a smooth, fierce thrust that thrilled her to the core.

'I hurt you?' he gasped, but she shook her head vehemently her fingers drumming such a wild, demanding tattoo on his shoulders Roberto made love to her with joyous lack of inhibition, kissing her open mouth as he drove her relentlessly towards the summit she flew over at last before him, and he gave a great groaning sigh in the throes of his release and collapsed on her. They lay panting and winded, held fast in each other's arms, until a knock on the door brought Roberto off the bed to dive into the robe he'd torn from Katherine.

She pulled the sheet up to her chin and lay still, listening as Roberto gave instructions to a waiter. A suite which opened into a sitting room had its advantages, she thought with approval. Roberto had merely looked flushed and slightly tousled about the head to confront the waiter while she probably looked like a wreck. She leapt to her feet to escape into the bathroom, but Roberto caught her and swept her up in his arms before she made it.

'It is too late to be shy, *carinha*!'

'I'm not shy.' Well, not much. 'I need another shower.'

'I will share it with you, *linda flor*. I have dreamed of this, also.' He set her down gently in the shower stall, threw off the robe and joined her.

Katherine half expected him to make love to her again once they were naked together, but Roberto merely held her close as the water streamed over them, then stepped out to fetch towels. He wrapped her in one of them, laughing as her stomach gave a sudden rumble.

'I hate to be unromantic,' she said wryly, 'but I'm hungry. I couldn't face much in the way of breakfast this morning.'

He gave her a searching look. 'You were sad to leave the Estancia?'

'Yes. It was hard to say goodbye.'

'I am pleased to hear that,' he informed her with satisfaction. 'Put on a robe while I dress, then we eat, *Doutora*.'

In underwear and robe, Katherine finger-combed her hair and followed Roberto into the sitting room, where their lunch waited on a table under the windows. With a flourish, Roberto removed a cover to display a vast colourful salad embedded with huge prawns.

'Wow!'

'So you see, English girl, we gauchos do not eat meat *all* the time.' He smiled. 'Come. Eat. You must renew your energy.'

Katherine raised an eyebrow and he pulled her close on the sofa beside him, chuckling as he kissed her cheek.

'I meant because you were so brave to fly here with me as pilot,' he assured her virtuously.

They enjoyed their long lazy lunch in front of windows with a spectacular view of the lagoon, the only cloud on Katherine's horizon the prospect that soon she must leave all this behind and go back to her normal life. But looking on the plus side, she reminded herself firmly, she had been given a glorious holiday with Roberto in a country she'd always longed to visit; though her preconception of Brazil had been mostly of Rio de Janeiro and Carnival, with minimal knowledge of the wide open spaces of gaucho country in Rio Grande do Sul, which she had come to love during her short stay. Riding out over his land with Roberto had been a deeply satisfying experience. She had enjoyed the camaraderie of his men, also achieved a close rapport with her horse.

'When you go back to the Estancia will you pat Garoto for me and tell him I'll miss him, Roberto?'

He took in a deep breath and then put their plates on the table and lifted her onto his lap. 'I need to hold you,' he said tersely, smoothing her head against his shoulder. Katherine relaxed against him, happy just to be alone with him in the quiet of the air-conditioned room, while the vibrant city life of Porto Alegre went on around them.

'When you say such things,' he said at last, his voice

husky, 'almost you make me cry. And it is not macho for a man to cry!'

'You take great pride in machismo?'

'*Pois e!* What man does not?' He gave her a crooked smile. 'When you left me in Portugal I wanted very much to cry, and exerted much self-control to avoid disillusioning Jorge.'

'I cried buckets,' she said frankly, and he laughed and hugged her close, but inwardly she shuddered. All too soon it would happen again when she flew home.

'Would you like tea, Katherine?'

She shook her head, stifling a yawn, and Roberto took her hand to pull her to her feet. '*Agora*. Now you rest.'

After the hectic programme of the past few days the idea was suddenly very appealing. 'But what will you do, Roberto?'

'I shall rest with you.' He looked surprised that she'd needed to ask. 'When you wake we shall drink tea and coffee, as we did many times in Quinta das Montanhas and at Estancia Grande, but here is better because we shall be in bed together. Not,' he said, his handsome face suddenly stern, 'that I will make love to you. You need sleep, Katherine. There are shadows under those beautiful green eyes. I will just hold your hand while you sleep, then later we go out on the town.'

She smiled drowsily and leaned back against the banked pillows. 'I loved Christmas at Estancia Grande, Roberto, but I'm so glad to be here alone with you for a while before I leave.'

He slid down beside her and raised her hand to his lips. 'It was a brilliant idea of mine, nao e?' He shifted slightly to look down into her eyes. 'Did your former lover object when you came here to me?'

'I didn't tell him. Andrew and I are no longer friends.'
Katherine pulled a face as she described the unpleasant
encounter in the flat.

Roberto lapsed into Portuguese to swear violently.
'He meant to force you?'

'I don't think he would have gone that far, but Hugh
and Alastair's arrival cut it short. At which point I told
Andrew it was over in front of witnesses—good move
because he's a lawyer—and said goodbye. I haven't seen
him since.'

'I would like to meet him,' said Roberto with quiet
menace.

'Unlikely that you will,' she pointed out.

'I will never force you, Katherine.'

She turned to smile at him. 'No need. One look
from you, Roberto Rocha de Sousa, and I melt in your
arms.'

'Amada!' He leant to kiss her swiftly, and then settled
beside her, holding her hand. 'Now close your eyes.
Dorme bem.'

Katherine woke alone later to the soft glow of lamps
from the open doorway to the other room. She shot up
to look at her watch as Roberto came to sit on the edge
of the bed.

'You feel rested now?' He bent to kiss her nose.

'I do, but I'm sorry I slept so long!'

'Nao importa, we eat later here in the city. Also you
were up very early almost every morning at the Estancia.
Tomorrow, you can have breakfast in bed.' He smoothed
her hair back with a caressing hand. 'I spoke with my
parents. My mother is glad we arrived safely, but feels
very sad now you are gone. I am commanded to ask you
to come back again soon.'

'How sweet of her.' Katherine felt enormous relief

that Roberto's parents had been so friendly. She had never been invited to meet a man's parents before, mainly because she'd deliberately kept her former relationships too casual for the question to arise. 'It was very good of your parents to invite a total stranger to their home for Christmas, Roberto.'

His eyebrows rose. 'You were my guest, not a stranger, Katherine. They were both eager to meet the clever lady who revealed my painting as a Gainsborough. And because of its provenance, she will always be grateful to you.'

She shook her head in wonder. 'I had no idea when I took James Massey's place that I would not only meet a star of the racing circuit—'

'Who you had never heard of,' he growled.

'True, but due to the joys of technology I soon found out! As I was saying, I had no idea that I would meet a sports celebrity who owned a Gainsborough, let alone that the subject of the painting would be his ancestor.' She met his eyes squarely. 'Nor that my client would be the most attractive man I'd ever met in my life.'

Roberto's eyes widened. 'Is that what you thought that first day? Even though I limped and had a scar?'

'Yes.' Her eyes flashed. 'While you were furious because I wasn't a man, and took one look at my clothes and spectacles and dismissed me as a frump.'

'Frump? What is that?'

'Someone who looked like me that day.'

He grinned and threw out his hands. 'To me, you seemed so blazingly intellectual you scared me greatly, *Doutora*. But you are also beautiful and compassionate and so looked past my injuries to the man underneath.'

Not quite. Dr Katherine Lister had simply taken one

look and fallen head over heels in love with the client just the way he was, scars and all. But until she was sure that Roberto's heart was involved in his feelings for her she would keep that to herself.

Lit up by night, Porto Alegre was even more exciting. Katherine held Roberto's hand in the taxi on the drive to the restaurant, in constant need of his touch as the time drew nearer to leave him. She pushed the thought away as they arrived at the Italian restaurant Roberto had chosen as a change for Katherine. Not that the location mattered to her. Roberto for companion was the important thing. She would willingly have stayed at the hotel and ordered room service again but, knowing he wanted her to experience some Porto Alegre night life, she had worn the green dress again and, with the emerald pendant and earrings to transform it, felt as beautiful as Roberto constantly told her she was.

The restaurant was intimate and sophisticated, the red wine was mellow and Roberto held her hand as much as possible throughout the meal as he outlined their itinerary for the next day before her flight.

'We will go shopping for these presents you must buy, Katherine.' He flung up a hand. 'And do not flash those eyes at me—I will not try to pay for them. Though if I find something you would like for yourself I *will* pay.'

'Roberto, you've gone to enormous expense to bring me here, no more presents are necessary,' she said firmly, and suddenly looked wistful. 'I had such gorgeous Christmas gifts from you and your parents, but I won't get much opportunity to wear them.'

'You must wear jewellery when you go out with friends?'

She laughed, and touched a hand to the pendant and earrings. 'True. But not like these. I shall keep them for special occasions.' She sighed. 'And the gaucho outfit will be just a souvenir. I ride in pretty ordinary gear at home. When I do, which is very seldom these days.'

'It looks very good on you, *amada*.' He raised her hand to his lips, oblivious of the other diners. 'And you should keep up the riding. Did you enjoy riding with me?'

'You know I did, Roberto. The entire holiday has been a wonderful experience.'

'It is not over yet, *querida*.' He summoned a waiter, paid the bill, then stood up and held out his hand. 'Come, Katherine. Let us find a taxi.'

Back at the hotel, it seemed like the most natural thing in the world to get ready for bed together, and then slide into each other's arms as though this was something they'd done every night for years.

Katherine smiled as she told Roberto this and he nodded in full agreement.

'I felt this from almost the first time I saw you.'

'You mean a bit later than that, after I scrubbed up and lost the glasses!'

'*E verdade!*' He laughed and hugged her closer. 'I was determined to have you, Katherine Lister, no matter how many men you'd left behind in England.'

She gave him a dig in the ribs. 'There was precisely one! Whereas you've had countless women in your life, Roberto de Sousa!'

'Mariana was the only one of significance.' He switched on a lamp and looked into her eyes. 'You are different. In my dreams I had always longed to meet a woman who appealed to my mind as well as my body. I had given up all hope of this—then I met you.' He kissed her with sudden, fierce possession, his hands moving in a demanding glissade down her spine to mould her against that part of him that sought entry, and her thighs parted for him in ardent welcome as he united their bodies in the earthy, heart-stopping intensity of rapture she knew she would never know again once they parted.

Roberto raised his head as his breathing slowed, consternation in his eyes as he saw her face. 'You are crying! Why?'

She swiped her tears away impatiently, about to lie, then changed her mind. 'Because I'm leaving you to-morrow.' She bit her quivering lower lip so hard Roberto frowned and placed soft, sweet kisses along her mouth to soothe it, then turned on his side and drew her against him.

'I know too well you are leaving me, so now we talk.'

Katherine looked up into his taut, determined face, and drew in a shaky breath. 'I'm sorry to spoil things by crying. Normally, I don't do tears much.' And all the tears she'd shed recently had been over Roberto de Sousa.

'I know this.' He stroked her hair back from her fore-head. 'At the thought of parting with you I want to cry myself.' He sighed. 'But men do not cry, of course.'

She managed a grin. 'Especially gaucho men!'

'That is better, *carinha*. I prefer your smiles to your tears.'

'So do I,' she said dryly. 'So what do you want to talk about, Roberto?'

'Myself, of course—what else would a man want to talk about?' he teased, then sobered. 'I want you to listen very carefully to me, Katherine. And stay close while I talk.'

Katherine had no intention of moving even a hair's

breadth. His warmth and nearness were a vital necessity as she braced herself to listen.

'When Luis died,' he began, 'I naturally returned immediately to the Estancia to comfort my parents. But because I want truth between us, Katherine, I confess that I did not intend to stay very long. Because I had been living away from home for years I had seen my family only on short visits for special reasons like Christmas and anniversaries. Because it was some months since I had seen him, it was a shock to find that my father was looking so much older. Because my mother is many years younger than him, the change in her was not so great.

'So Roberto Rocha, darling of the racing circuit, decided to take a sabbatical from his career and stay at the Estancia to lighten some of his father's load. Because he had been born to it, he was soon so much part of life on Estancia Grande he began taking over from his grieving father more and more. But he never lost sight of the ultimate goal—that once his father had overcome his grief Roberto Rocha would return to his life on the track for a few years until it was the natural time to retire and return to his roots.

'Then I went to a friend's wedding, met Elena, and was moron enough to throw myself into my car to prevent her stealing it,' said Roberto with disgust. 'All thoughts of a career ended. I worked hard to recover physically, but mentally I was…how do you say …wallowing in self-pity. Then fate sent Dr Katherine Lister into my life and changed it for ever.' He turned her face up to his and kissed her to emphasize the point. 'When my father took me to the hospital straight from the airport I was ready to endure anything the doctors could do to help me walk and ride normally.'

Katherine smoothed a hand over his hard chest. 'Was the pain terrible, Roberto?'

'For a while, yes, but I did whatever was asked of me to begin recovering.' He lifted her hand to his lips. 'But I could not ring you until I knew for certain that I would be able to function normally, both in the saddle and on two feet.'

'You could have asked someone to send me an email, so I at least knew you'd arrived safely,' she pointed out.

'I preferred to wait until I could hear your voice, Katherine,' he said flatly. 'I had much time to think about what my life would be once I was home on the Estancia for good. And though I love my parents, and enjoy the company of men, I needed more in my life. I so much missed you, *amada* I asked you here for Christmas, hoping that you would enjoy a stay on the Estancia.'

'Which I did,' she sighed.

'You took to the life like...you have a phrase about ducks?'

'Like a duck to water?'

'*Isso.* To ride out with you on Garoto by my side brought me much joy.'

'Me too,' she said huskily.

Roberto turned her face up to his. 'Then I have a question to ask.' His eyes, darkly brilliant with an emotion which started her heart beating like a drum, locked with hers. 'Do you love me, Katherine?'

It wasn't the question she'd been hoping for, but she burnt some of her boats and answered it anyway. 'Yes. I do.'

He let out a deep unsteady breath and kissed her until

her head reeled. '*Gracas a Deus,*' he said against her mouth. 'How I have longed to hear you say that.'

'Why?' she demanded.

'You must know why!'

Katherine looked deep into the dark, possessive eyes and burnt the last of her boats. 'Is it by any chance because you love me?'

'You have to ask?' he said in astonishment. 'I thought it was written across my forehead for all to see.'

Her eyes fell, as her heart thumped so loudly she was sure he must be able to hear it. 'I knew only too well you wanted me—physically, I mean.'

'And I do,' he assured her with passion. 'I adore your body, but even more I love you with all my heart and soul and always will. So will you marry me and live in the land of the gaucho with me for ever, Katherine? Because if you say yes it must mean until death parts us.'

'I do say yes. To almost everything,' she added, to avoid any misunderstanding.

'Almost?' he said warily.

'I've been on my own for a long time, and I'm used to running my life the way I want it. And although I would enjoy life on the Estancia, Roberto, I'm accustomed to earning my own living. I'd like to carry on with my job. With the wonder of technology, I could work for James wherever I am.'

'I will buy you the ultimate in computers so you can do that, I promise,' he said emphatically. 'And if you miss your life in London you shall invite your friends to stay whenever you wish—but not the lawyer! So, Dr Lister. Will you marry me?'

She smiled at him radiantly. 'Yes, Senhor Sousa, I will.'

Roberto held her close in passionate thanksgiving, and then got out of bed to make for his overnight bag. As he slid back beside her he held out his hand. 'This is not a present, Katherine. This is a token of my love. Will you accept it?'

She looked at the emerald and diamond ring lying on his palm and blinked away tears. This was no time to be crying! 'Oh, Roberto! It's glorious. Of course I'll accept it.'

'I bought it with the other pieces,' he informed her as he slid it on the appropriate finger, 'but before I could offer it to you it was necessary to wait until you had more experience of what life with me would mean.' He raised her hand and kissed the ring, then gave her an imperious look. 'Do not make me wait long before we add a wedding band, *querida*. We have spent too many years of our lives apart. It is time that we were together, as fate intended.'

EPILOGUE

MOONLIGHT bathed the gardens with its usual magic at Quinta das Montanhas when Katherine joined the man leaning against a pillar to wait for her. Roberto de Sousa took her in his arms and kissed her with rather more reverence than she had expected in such circumstances.

'*Minha esposa*,' he said against her lips. 'At last you are my wife.'

Katherine sighed happily. 'We finally made it. Now all we need is a *churrasco* party at Estancia Grande when we get home, to celebrate the deed, and I'll feel we're well and truly married.'

Roberto laughed softly. 'I know easier—and more delightful—ways to convince you of that!'

'I bet you do, Roberto Rocha!'

'*I* was not the one who gave that name to the photographers at our wedding, *querida*!'

She sighed. 'I know. Who knew Hugh would be so sneaky? Sorry about that.'

'On such a day, why would I mind?' Roberto kissed her again, the reverence less in evidence this time. 'But that was yesterday, and my bride was so tired last night I—saint that I am—let her sleep in peace. But now Lidia and Jorge have served us a sumptuous wedding supper and vanished to their quarters, come, *minha mulher*, let us do the same.' He held out his hand. 'I can carry you upstairs if you wish, but it is better I keep my energy for more important activities, *nao e*?'

'Absolutely,' she assured him as they went hand in hand up the familiar staircase. Roberto picked her up to carry her inside the bedroom she'd slept in before, and set her down to undress her with urgent hands before laying her on the bed.

'*Amada*,' he said huskily, as they lay naked together for the first time as man and wife. 'I have so longed for this day—and this night. I need much consolation for all the nights we have spent apart.'

Katherine gladly provided it, putting all the pent up longing of their separation into her kisses as Roberto made passionate love to her with hungry lips and urgent hands until their bodies could no longer exist apart. As they came together as man and wife for the first time, tears hung on Katherine's lashes as Roberto told her in two languages how much he adored and cherished her, and how happy she made him, until at last there was only the sound of their sobbing breaths as they surged together to a climax that left them speechless in each other's arms.

Roberto raised his head at last, his eyes luminous in the moonlight streaming through the window. 'Look at me, Katherine.'

She raised heavy eyelids to gaze up into the taut, handsome face, marvelling that she was really here, in her bridegroom's arms at long last. 'I'm looking,' she whispered.

'I swear I will make you happy, always.'

'I am happy. A happily married woman,' she added in wonder. 'But I had to get through a surprising amount of work to achieve it, not least organising things with the house.'

'It is good your friends are renting it from you,' he agreed, and rolled on his back, pulling her close. 'They wished to buy it, no?'

Katherine nodded. 'But I could never sell it.'

'It would cause pain to sever your link with your father,' agreed Roberto.

She reached up and kissed him, grateful for his perception. 'Yes. But I have the comfort of knowing it's in good hands. Hugh is still renting the top flat, and I was happy to let Alastair and Rachel turn the two lower floors into one for their first home. Sam Napier will make sure the conversion is done well.'

'I liked him very much, Charlotte, too. She is a most elegant lady.'

'But your mother stole the show in that fabulous hat.' Katherine chuckled drowsily. 'I'm so pleased she braved the flight to see us married.'

'I will tell her that when I ring the Estancia after they return home.' Roberto smoothed the hair back from her face. 'James Massey told me he is happy about the new arrangement with you.'

She nodded happily. 'With the aid of my spanking new computer I can work for him from Estancia Grande as easily as I can at the gallery.'

'Do not let the computer take up all your time, *amada*.' He rolled onto his side to look into her eyes. 'Save most of it for me.'

'I will,' she assured him.

'Ah, *querida*, do you know how I felt when you made your vows to me?'

'Pleased? Happy?'

'*De certeza*. But it was more than that. When I was

racing I believed that the only thing important was to be world champion.' He drew her close. 'I was wrong. To win you as my wife is the greatest achievement of my life. Why are you crying, *amada*?'

'How can you expect me not to when you say things like that to me?' She blinked the tears from her lashes and smiled into his eyes. 'If it's any consolation, Roberto Rocha, you'll always be world champion as far as I'm concerned. If we had a bottle of champagne handy I'd spray it all over you to prove it.'

Roberto gave a delighted laugh and hugged her close. 'There is something I would like more than champagne.'

'What is it?'

'This is our wedding night, *querida*, so make a guess!'

'If you mean you want to make love to me again, take me, I'm yours!' she assured him, smiling. Her smile faded. 'I mean that, Roberto. I've been yours from the moment I first set eyes on you, whether you wanted me or not.'

His eyes lit with the smile which always made her heart beat faster. 'Of course I wanted you, *amada*. While I breathe I always will. And now I have you, *minha esposa*, I will never let you go!'

* * * * *

AUGUST 2011 HARDBACK TITLES

ROMANCE

Bride for Real	Lynne Graham
From Dirt to Diamonds	Julia James
The Thorn in His Side	Kim Lawrence
Fiancée for One Night	Trish Morey
The Untamed Argentinian	Susan Stephens
After the Greek Affair	Chantelle Shaw
The Highest Price to Pay	Maisey Yates
Under the Brazilian Sun	Catherine George
There's Something About a Rebel...	Anne Oliver
The Crown Affair	Lucy King
Australia's Maverick Millionaire	Margaret Way
Rescued by the Brooding Tycoon	Lucy Gordon
Not-So-Perfect Princess	Melissa McClone
The Heart of a Hero	Barbara Wallace
Swept Off Her Stilettos	Fiona Harper
Mr Right There All Along	Jackie Braun
The Tortured Rebel	Alison Roberts
Dating Dr Delicious	Laura Iding

HISTORICAL

Married to a Stranger	Louise Allen
A Dark and Brooding Gentleman	Margaret McPhee
Seducing Miss Lockwood	Helen Dickson
The Highlander's Return	Marguerite Kaye

MEDICAL™

The Doctor's Reason to Stay	Dianne Drake
Career Girl in the Country	Fiona Lowe
Wedding on the Baby Ward	Lucy Clark
Special Care Baby Miracle	Lucy Clark

AUGUST 2011
LARGE PRINT TITLES

ROMANCE

Jess's Promise	Lynne Graham
Not For Sale	Sandra Marton
After Their Vows	Michelle Reid
A Spanish Awakening	Kim Lawrence
In the Australian Billionaire's Arms	Margaret Way
Abby and the Bachelor Cop	Marion Lennox
Misty and the Single Dad	Marion Lennox
Daycare Mum to Wife	Jennie Adams

HISTORICAL

Miss in a Man's World	Anne Ashley
Captain Corcoran's Hoyden Bride	Annie Burrows
His Counterfeit Condesa	Joanna Fulford
Rebellious Rake, Innocent Governess	Elizabeth Beacon

MEDICAL™

Cedar Bluff's Most Eligible Bachelor	Laura Iding
Doctor: Diamond in the Rough	Lucy Clark
Becoming Dr Bellini's Bride	Joanna Neil
Midwife, Mother...Italian's Wife	Fiona McArthur
St Piran's: Daredevil, Doctor...Dad!	Anne Fraser
Single Dad's Triple Trouble	Fiona Lowe

SEPTEMBER 2011
HARDBACK TITLES

ROMANCE

The Kanellis Scandal	Michelle Reid
Monarch of the Sands	Sharon Kendrick
One Night in the Orient	Robyn Donald
His Poor Little Rich Girl	Melanie Milburne
The Sultan's Choice	Abby Green
The Return of the Stranger	Kate Walker
Girl in the Bedouin Tent	Annie West
Once Touched, Never Forgotten	Natasha Tate
Nice Girls Finish Last	Natalie Anderson
The Italian Next Door...	Anna Cleary
From Daredevil to Devoted Daddy	Barbara McMahon
Little Cowgirl Needs a Mum	Patricia Thayer
To Wed a Rancher	Myrna Mackenzie
Once Upon a Time in Tarrula	Jennie Adams
The Secret Princess	Jessica Hart
Blind Date Rivals	Nina Harrington
Cort Mason – Dr Delectable	Carol Marinelli
Survival Guide to Dating Your Boss	Fiona McArthur

HISTORICAL

The Lady Gambles	Carole Mortimer
Lady Rosabella's Ruse	Ann Lethbridge
The Viscount's Scandalous Return	Anne Ashley
The Viking's Touch	Joanna Fulford

MEDICAL ROMANCE™

Return of the Maverick	Sue MacKay
It Started with a Pregnancy	Scarlet Wilson
Italian Doctor, No Strings Attached	Kate Hardy
Miracle Times Two	Josie Metcalfe

0811 Gen Std LP

SEPTEMBER 2011
LARGE PRINT TITLES

ROMANCE

Too Proud to be Bought	Sharon Kendrick
A Dark Sicilian Secret	Jane Porter
Prince of Scandal	Annie West
The Beautiful Widow	Helen Brooks
Rancher's Twins: Mum Needed	Barbara Hannay
The Baby Project	Susan Meier
Second Chance Baby	Susan Meier
Her Moment in the Spotlight	Nina Harrington

HISTORICAL

More Than a Mistress	Ann Lethbridge
The Return of Lord Conistone	Lucy Ashford
Sir Ashley's Mettlesome Match	Mary Nichols
The Conqueror's Lady	Terri Brisbin

MEDICAL ROMANCE™

Summer Seaside Wedding	Abigail Gordon
Reunited: A Miracle Marriage	Judy Campbell
The Man with the Locked Away Heart	Melanie Milburne
Socialite...or Nurse in a Million?	Molly Evans
St Piran's: The Brooding Heart Surgeon	Alison Roberts
Playboy Doctor to Doting Dad	Sue MacKay